s m nostrini

PLANTAGENET TRILOGY - BOOK TWO

SETH'S SOLACE

WHERE WILL HIS HELP COME FROM?

Ark House Press
PO Box 1722, Port Orchard, WA 98366 USA
PO Box 1321, Mona Vale NSW 1660 Australia
PO Box 318 334, West Harbour, Auckland 0661 New Zealand
arkhousepress.com

All Bible verse references are taken from the New International Version.

Disclaimer: This is a work of fiction, names, characters, events and incidences are either the products of the author's imagination or used in a fictitious manner. Any resemblance to actual persons living or dead, or actual events is purely coinci-dental. The town of Mt Barker and surrounding districts are real.

Cataloguing in Publication Data:
Title: Seth's Solace: Book 2 Plantagenet Trilogy
ISBN: 978-0-6489380-5-7 (pbk)
Subjects: Christian Fiction; Historical Romance;

Design by initiateagency.com

In honour of our
red cloud Kelpie,
Nuffy

ACKNOWLEDGEMENTS

Where does my help come from? Most importantly, the Maker of heaven and earth. It is a blessing and honour to have discovered the joy of writing and sharing God's message in the form of a novel. I appreciate the support and encouragement of Audrey Payne, Sharron Wise and Alison Inglis who give of their time to read and proof my work. You are wonderful ladies and offer different points of view that help to grow the story to its fullness.

Special thanks to my niece's husband, Damon Lawrence, for his appraisal of the essence of *Seth's Solace*. Writing from a man's perspective, and the emotions experienced in his pain meant I needed the reassurance of understanding from one who has walked a similar path. Thanks Damo!

Thank you Nicole and James, and their team from Initiate Media. God bless you and grant you rest in your busyness.

I would like to acknowledge the Noongar Menang people on whose land this book was written.

COURTNEY'S KEYS

BOOK ONE IN THE PLANTAGENET TRILOGY

Bewildered by a chequered past and rattled by poor decisions, twenty year-old Courtney Lancaster discovers keys that reveal resolutions to her confusion. Trials and temptations create stumbling blocks along the way. Can she confront the one issue that persists on knocking at her heart's door?

Raised as a ward-of-the-state in the Australian state of New South Wales, she becomes the beneficiary of an unknown relative. She arrives in Mt Barker, in the south-west of Western Australia, to discover treasures from her past. A new beginning allows Courtney to learn life lessons from a trustworthy neighbour and growing faith in a loving God. But the secret she is concealing, once exposed, will change everything.

Plantagenet Trilogy – Book One

CHARACTER LIST FROM COURTNEY'S KEYS:

Mt Barker:

Courtney Lancaster

Liam Wilson

Millie Lockridge

Todd York

Rev. Bob and Beryl Webber

Geoffrey Lancaster

Michael and Claire Lancaster

Frankland River:

Keith Crawford

Tom and Annie O'Reilly

Jimmy, Jon and Bronte O'Reilly

Freya Carlisle

Sydney:

Jacob Hoyle

Perth:

Kate Smythe

Jerry Keller

CHAPTER 1

Cranbrook, Western Australia

July, 1981

Dawn. A wash of pale oyster-grey light revealed shadowy hills on the horizon. Mist swirled within the hollows. Dew droplets adorned intricate gossamer cobwebs on native scrub along the gravel boundary road. Snug in his swag, Seth lingered in the cosy warmth. He wore a beanie pulled down tight over his head and ears, only his face felt the cool air at the break of day. This is all too good to be true, he thought. *Silence, space, creation and an escape from reality.*

Mallee, his faithful red cloud Kelpie, was curled up beside him sound asleep. The campfire emitted a little warmth from a mound of coals within a ring of paddock rocks. It wouldn't take much to stoke it up though, and boil the billy.

The sheep farmer stood, stretched his tall frame and rubbed his hand over the stubble on his face. He added a few sticks to the coals. After a snap and crackle of the kindling, a flame ignited and the fire revived. The dog sniffed around a bush and relieved herself before she returned to sit beside her master. The pair shared burnt toast cooked on a toasting fork over the fire while pungent bacon sizzled in the frying pan and baked beans warmed in a pot. Seth sipped sweet black tea from his hot billy, satisfied after his breakfast.

Psalm 23 came to mind; 'The Lord is *my* shepherd, I shall not be in want. He makes me lie down in green pastures, he leads me beside still waters. He restores my soul.' Seth looked across the paddock to the sheep with lambs cavorting at their mothers' sides; he took in the green feed, and noticed the weak morning sunlight kiss the chalk-coloured water in the dam.

Seth prayed quietly within his soul. *Lord, you are my shepherd, and you bless me. Even through the tough times you're always there. You're my strength and give me comfort. I just hope that things with Felicity will work themselves out.* His prayer came from the heart but negative thoughts nagged at the back of his mind.

Cold air bit into his hands. He paused to rub them together and circulate some warmth. Seth pulled on leather gloves but his hands still felt numb while he fumbled with the pliers and twisted the wire. An hour later his body began to thaw from the energy it took to do the work and the sunshine that peeked through the clouds.

The south boundary fence had needed replacing a long time ago to keep his flock within the property. Seth took to the job after seeding a crop for hay-making. There had been early winter rains, and healthy green shoots poked through the brown overturned soil.

Strainer posts creaked as they bore the tug of tension on the galvanised wire when he completed the length of fencing. The ring-lock wire had been unrolled and pinned to the posts dotted along the way as far as he could see. Barbed wire was strung along the top row. Seth pulled his gloves off to stretch his fingers but then noticed a kink in a wire tie. He reached across to straighten it and caught the back of his hand on a barb. A bright red strip of blood appeared.

"Should've left my gloves on," he muttered wiping at it with a hankie to stem the flow. He looked at the wound and felt his life had been like that lately. Bleeding and painful.

"Come on, Mallee girl. Let's get that gate off the ute."

Seth turned the final bolt into the hinge fitting and drew the chain across to secure the farm gate. He stood back and admired his week's work where the kilometres of new fence disappeared into the distance.

"Okay, we can head home now."

The dog cocked her ears. 'Home'. That meant a ride back to the house. Her intelligent eyes lit up and she followed him with a spring in her step. The Stirling Ranges were no longer visible, a drizzle of rain masked their presence. Good timing, he thought. Ash flicked up out of the fire pit when he threw water on the cooled embers. The fencing and camping gear was loaded on board.

"Hop up, Mallee." With an energetic leap the dog went to her favoured spot behind the driver's seat on the back of the ute. Holding a solid stance with her dark reddish-brown face pointed directly into the breeze, they flew along the two-wheel track to the homestead.

Seth checked the time. It was just past two o'clock, he'd had a quick ham and mustard sandwich and gone to the study to do some book work. He stood for a break; there was time to do a bit more but he needed to clear his head. A mocking laugh caught his attention. He glanced out the window to where a pair of kookaburras sat in the huge gum tree belting out their unique chorus. He smiled. The kids loved to copy with their own version of 'koo koo koo kah kah kah.' Ryan had almost mastered a true sound, but Alicia's attempts were funny little noises that didn't much resemble a kookaburra's laugh. His mind wandered into prayer.

Lord, bless and protect my children. Help Ryan learn to trust people, and thank you that he had enough confidence to go for a sleep-over. I pray for Alicia, thank you that she helps her big brother like she does. She surprises me with her ability to interpret his feelings and knows what he needs, and when he needs it.

Ryan agreeing to stay over with friends was a huge achievement for his son. He looked forward to hearing all about it when he'd pick them up later. Seth appreciated the opportunity to spend the night out in the paddock by himself. It was a treasured time of solitude and renewal of inner strength. Little did he know the foreboding he felt that morning was an omen of what was to come.

Six months earlier ...

"Have you got everything you need for your swimming lessons?" Seth called out to his six-year-old daughter and eight-year-old son from the bedroom.

"Yes, Dad." Alicia rolled her eyes. Of course, she did. She'd checked Ryan's bag too.

"We've got our towels, goggles, sunscreen and water bottles. And dry undies for afterwards. We're wearing our bathers under our shorts and T-shirts." The little girl paused to think about anything she might have forgotten.

"Oh, we should take a plastic bag for our wet things when we get changed. I'll get them from the pantry."

She scooted off to the kitchen, found the calico bag stuffed with David Jones black and white shopping bags and pulled two out. Alicia skipped down the passageway to put one in her bag and one in her brother's bag as well. She couldn't wait, Dad was taking them to their swimming lessons this year. Ryan sat on the floor building something out of Lego blocks, oblivious to his sister's banter.

"Right, time to go."

Seth came into the lounge room with a large suitcase and a beaming smile on his face.

"What's the case for?"

Alicia frowned, maybe Dad wasn't coming with them after all.

"I've got a surprise for you."

Both children looked at their father, he had their attention now.

"We're going to have a little holiday for the next two weeks in Mt Barker."

"Really?"

Ryan jumped up and wrapped his arms around Seth's legs.

"With you, you mean?"

The boys clear pale green eyes locked with the matching eyes looking down at him.

"Yes, son. The three of us, we're staying at a guest house and we'll have our meals cooked for us and everything."

Alicia jumped up and down on the spot.

"Goodie, goodie. What else are we going to do while we're there?"

"Well, we'll go to your swimming lessons every morning. Then go out for lunch at a cafe or have a picnic; maybe we could stay at the pool, find a playground or play some games. Whatever you'd like to do. We have to come home on the weekend though, just to check the animals and make sure everything's okay."

"Who's going to look after the chooks and the dog while we're not here?"

Concern wrinkled Alicia's little forehead, dampening her excitement.

"Fred from up the road will do that for us during the week. I've already made the arrangements. Come on, we don't want to be late on the first day. Let's go."

Once Alicia was assured that her chickens and Mallee were going to be looked after, the trio made their way out to the vehicle parked in the driveway and off they went.

Cool air flowed through the breeze blocks in the corridor while the father and his children waited in the queue to enter the swimming pool. It was a welcome relief from the heat of the day. Women and children of various ages milled around the edges of the fenced pool area. Teachers with peaked caps and sunglasses held clipboards with class lists, and checked off student names as they assembled for the lesson.

They found Ryan's teacher and he joined a group of three boys and two girls. His class was before Alicia's, so father and daughter looked around to find a spot under the shade-cloth shelters to settle themselves where they could watch Ryan.

Alicia spread out her Barbie beach towel and put her things down on it. Seth sat beside her. On the grass next to them a bassinet held a sleeping baby, and a young red-haired girl rested against her mother's arm. He smiled at the woman.

"Hello," she responded to Seth's smile. "I'm Annie,' she looked at Alicia, 'and this is Bronte."

"Hi, Bronte."

The shy girl smiled but remained beside her mum. Alicia chatted to Bronte in her usual friendly manner explaining how her Nanna had given her the towel and matching bathers for Christmas. Her brother had Teenage Mutant Ninja Turtle board shorts and a towel with Donatello on it, and their Dad's towel had a palm tree on a tropical island. It didn't take long for Bronte to thaw out and soon the girls were playing together in and around the adults.

Annie couldn't help sneaking a look at the tall man with light-brown hair. His eyes were fascinating. Such a pale green, they were almost translucent. Seth noticed. It wasn't uncommon for people to be interested in the colour of his eyes. He ignored the attention. It could be that he was the only man at the pool; he did feel somewhat conspicuous.

Ryan arrived with his towel wrapped around him, lips blue even though the day was hot. He plonked himself down between his Dad's bent knees. Seth hugged the boy to warm him up.

"Five minutes, Alicia, and you need to get ready for your lesson," Seth reminded her.

"Okay, Dad." She sat down and took a hairbrush and covered elastic band out of her bag.

"Can you tie my hair back, please, Dad?"

He adeptly brushed her long dark honey-coloured hair. It caught copper highlights in the sunshine.

"Remember not to pull it up."

"I know, Alicia. I'll do it just how you like."

Seth looked across to Annie who'd taken in the exchange.

"She has to have her neck covered," Seth explained.

Annie nodded, smiling.

"Where do I go, Dad?"

"I'm coming with you."

Ryan stayed behind while Seth headed off to find Alicia's teacher. Two of the boys in his class came back to their mum, they were Bronte's brothers.

"Boys, stay here with the baby while I take Bronte to her lesson. Don't leave until I get back, okay?"

She eyed them both to make sure they heard her.

"Yes, Mum." They said in unison.

One of them spoke to Ryan.

"You're in our class."

Ryan nodded.

"We're twins. I'm Jimmy and this is Jon. He wears the blue and red boardies and I have the ones with pink and yellow flowers on 'em. Can't believe Mum makes me wear flowers.

"They are hibiscus, and they're trendy, Jimmy."

He hadn't realised his mum heard what he said.

"Anyway, you don't tell people to identify you by what you're wearing."

"Yeah, but we don't want to get called the wrong name. Can we have something to eat, Mum?"

Jimmy was always hungry. Annie looked at the boy and waited. He knew what that 'look' meant.

"Please ..." he said with a tilt of his head.

Annie gave the boys an apple and some biscuits. She offered Ryan some but he refused.

"Come on, Ryan, come with us."

Ryan hesitated. He looked at his father standing beside him who nodded in ascent, but the boy shook his head.

"Maybe in a little while, boys. Thanks, though."

Seth didn't force his son to go with them.

Annie looked at Ryan and noticed his eyes were the same colour as his father's. Intriguing.

"Sorry, I've been staring. I've never seen green eyes like yours before. Bronte's are green but they're a deeper colour with a dark grey ring around the iris."

"I got called 'cat's eyes' a lot when I was a kid. Fortunately, Ryan doesn't get any of that." Seth brushed his hand over his son's blonde head. "Apparently there's a lot less melanin pigment granules in the iris which makes the colouring so different."

"That sounds very technical," Annie chuckled through her comment. The baby stirred and started to whimper. "Oh, it's time for a feed."

Annie pulled a bottle of milk out of the nappy bag and tested the temperature on her wrist.

"Perfect."

She reached over and picked up the tiny baby who quieted as soon as the teat met its mouth.

"You are such a good girl," Annie cooed to the little one while she fed.

So it's a girl, Seth thought. The child was wrapped in a white bunny rug and it was a bit hard to tell from that. He was surprised to see the baby was quite different from the other children. You could tell Bronte and her brothers were related. The infant was olive-skinned and had a shock of black hair. *Maybe this child has a different father?*

"This is my granddaughter, Kaimarie. She's only two weeks old."

Annie must have heard him thinking. Seth was embarrassed. Maybe he was transparent enough that she realised his query.

"You don't look old enough to be a grandmother."

"I'm not, or rather I shouldn't be ..." Annie left that thought hanging. She paused but was compelled to continue. "My daughter is 18, and I had her when I was 16. All a bit of a shame, really. Freya, my daughter, didn't want this baby. By the time she realised she was pregnant, it was too late for an abortion. Thank the Lord; she knew I wouldn't approve of that choice and she couldn't be bothered with the adoption processes. Her solution to the problem was to come to us and have the baby here."

What was it about this man that made her feel comfortable enough to tell someone she didn't know these things? Annie felt she might as well go on now.

"Freya refused to feed her and a week later, on New Year's Day, she left. I found a note in the bassinet to say she knew I would take good care of the baby. She didn't even give her a name."

Annie's voice cracked with emotion, her eyes glazed over with unshed tears. Seth felt for the woman sitting beside him. He understood her pain.

"We decided to call her Kaimarie. The Kai part of her name is Hawaiian - meaning 'from the sea'. The boys found it in a book of baby names we borrowed from the library. Bronte had a special friend in Perth whose name was Marie. She wanted to call the baby after her friend, so we put the two together.

"I think it suits her," Seth wasn't quite sure what he was supposed to say.

"Yes, it does. She's a good baby. She eats, sleeps and does all the right things. Very placid, thankfully. I've got enough on my plate with those two."

She looked across to where the boys were running around playing tag with each other, and yelling as they went.

Seth smiled. They were happy and healthy children. Ryan continued to watch the boys, twisting and turning his head to follow their antics.

"You can go and play," his father whispered in his ear.

Ryan responded with a shake of his head.

"Do you live in Mt Barker?" Annie asked.

"No, we have a farm near Cranbrook.[1] Ryan and Alicia usually go to their grandparents in Bunbury for swimming lessons, but my father-in-law had a heart attack and it's too much to expect them to run the kids around this year."

"Mmm. We moved from Perth to a winery at Frankland River a little while ago. My husband is the caretaker on the property. We love living in the country. One of the reasons I'm here is because Bronte nearly drowned in the dam. She's not confident near the water now. It frightened the life out of Tom and me, and we decided she has to learn to swim properly."

The baby burped as Annie rubbed her back.

"Good girl." Annie laughed. "We congratulate them when they burp at this age, then later on we have to teach them its rude."

Seth smiled at the irony of her comment.

Alicia held Bronte's hand as they walked back after their lesson. They were in different groups, but next to each other in the pool.

"Bronte was a bit scared in her class, Dad. So I kept smiling at her and she got better."

"Thank you, Alicia, that was kind of you." Annie was impressed at the young girl's maturity. "We have to pack up and head off home straight away today. Come on boys," she called Jimmy and Jon back. "Maybe we'll see you tomorrow."

---

1 *Cranbrook*, history (see Afterword)

Seth sent Alicia and Ryan off to the showers to get washed up and changed. He sat alone on the grass while he watched people leave, and saw others arrive for the next set of lessons. Annie's story swam in his head, he couldn't fathom how any mother could leave her children. It just wasn't what was supposed to happen, but it did.

He shook his head and pulled the car keys out of his pocket and pushed the thoughts aside. The children approached with their faces aglow, Seth wasn't sure if it was a touch of sunburn, or if it was from the sheer pleasure of being with him. He liked to think it was the latter.

CHAPTER 2

The distinct aroma of fish and chips wafting up stimulated their appetites when Seth tore a hole in the butcher's paper for them to dig out the hot food. Ryan dropped a chip, flicked his fingers and blew on them where they burned. He licked off the salt.

"Ow, Dad, can you take some out and let them cool a bit? Please?"

The kids were hungry after their swimming lesson and it had been a long time since breakfast. A debate about which drink they wanted had taken longer than anticipated. Seth thought there was no point in getting annoyed. It was part of the holiday fun. Ryan chose Fanta and Alicia got a Passiona. Seth had his usual ice-cold Coke. The picnic was enjoyed, and the children played on the swings while their father watched through half-closed eyes trying not to fall asleep in the warm afternoon sun.

"Ry," Alicia whispered to her brother, "let's sneak up on Dad and scare him."

Ryan smiled at his sister's suggestion. Their father had just about nodded off and Alicia thought he wasn't watching them. They tiptoed toward the tree where Seth had propped himself into a comfortable position. A twig broke underfoot, and they froze, but the snapping sound didn't seem to disturb the almost-asleep man. A sudden rush and roar of noise besieged Seth and he responded with the appropriate fright for the playfulness of his kids. He grabbed them and tickled the pair to make them laugh until they nearly cried.

"Time to go," he announced.

They packed up and headed to Lancaster Guest House.

Courtney greeted them at the door and ushered them into the kitchen. Introductions were made and the family sat at the dining room table. A jug of lime cordial and glasses were put out with a plate of biscuits. They accepted a drink and chose a melting moment with a cream filling. The kids smiled at each other. This was going to be a good place to stay.

"Now, Jarvo, I want you to feel comfortable while you're here. Home away from home, if you like."

"That might not be such a good idea," Seth responded with a grimace on his face.

"Well, we're looking forward to getting to know you and the children."

Liam walked in and the men shook hands.

"Jarvo, welcome."

"Dad, how come they call you Jarvo?" Alicia asked outright. "Your name is Seth." Courtney and Liam looked at each other with widened eyes.

"I don't like people to call you Jarvo."

Courtney's hand made its way to cover her mouth.

"Alicia," her father's voice was an octave lower than normal with a warning edge to it.

"Sorry folks. I got the Jarvo label when I was in high school, you know, the proverbial sporting nickname. My name is Seth Jarvis. Feel free to call me Seth, if you want."

"That's such a nice name," Courtney offered smiling at Alicia.

The little girl beamed back at her. Ryan sat quietly, not contributing to the dialogue but not surprised by his sister's comments.

Liam showed them to the guest room and explained how they could come in the back door without having to go through the house. Liam left them to it. The room was comfortable and inviting with its shades of blue and polished wooden floorboards.

Seth collected the suitcase from the car, unpacked the clothes they'd brought with them and rinsed out the swimsuits. He hung them and the towels over the verandah railing to dry. Alicia and Ryan played UNO together while he did these jobs then they asked him to join in.

"Dad, did you bring our games Nanna and Pop gave us for Christmas?" Alicia asked.

"Yes, I did but they are still in the boot of the car. I'll go and get them."

Alicia didn't have a squabble with anyone over wanting the pink hippo, Ryan picked the orange one and Dad could choose either yellow or green. Hungry, Hungry Hippo ended up being a raucous, noisy game to play with hippo's chomping like crazy to see who could get the most balls. Vying to capture the only yellow ball for extra points created great competition.

Seth worried they were being too loud but realised at this time of the day it wouldn't matter. Afterwards, the kids decided to play the much quieter and more strategic game of Guess Who. They had a lot of fun trying to identify the opponents character. Only two people could play at a time, so Seth picked up his book and lay on the bed reading while he listened to the children.

"Does your person have a moustache?" Ryan asked.

"No."

Tiles were pushed down and Alicia had her turn.

"Is your person a lady?"

"Yes."

That eliminated a lot of faces. Ryan groaned. He needed a good question this time.

"Does your person have glasses?"

And they continued the search, game after game.

They really did get on well with each other and Seth was proud of them.

Dinner was going to be served at 6.00pm. They all got changed to go into the dining room but not before having a discussion about using table manners and watching what they said. Alicia got a look from her Dad as a reminder not to be too outspoken. She wriggled her shoulders in response and ran her tongue around the inside of her mouth. Seth had to look away so she couldn't see his suppressed smile.

They took their places at the table and Liam explained that they said grace before the meal. The hosts were surprised when the children immediately put their hands up and held onto each other. Everyone followed suit. Seth probably enjoyed the meal more than anyone else, and they didn't even have to help with the washing-up.

"That was nice, wasn't it, Dad?" Alicia mumbled with a mouthful of toothpaste as they readied for bed.

"It was great. What did you think, Ry?" his Dad asked.

"Yum. Courtney's a good cook."

"Especially the sweets." Alicia rubbed her tummy when she said this.

"Okay, prayers and off to bed."

It didn't take long for two children to be sound asleep. Seth returned to the dining room for the coffee he was offered when he was ready for it. The adults sat around and talked for a couple of hours about nothing in particular and everything in general. A yawn or two later and Seth excused himself and went off to his room.

After breakfast on Tuesday the family packed up for a day at the pool. They went to the bakery to buy sandwiches and got some fruit and biscuits from the Co-op for lunch. They were all set. Annie arrived a bit later but still managed to find a spot near Seth and the children.

Bronte and Alicia played with the dolls Annie brought to encourage the girls to stay in the shade. It was better for her daughter to be out of the sunshine as much as possible because of her fair skin. Swimming lessons went well and Seth jumped into the pool for a swim with the children. The twins had a ball and played with a much less shy Ryan.

Alicia was first out of the pool and lay on her towel to dry off. Seth shook his head and water droplets flicked over her back.

"Dad!" she shrieked. "I was just about dry."

They laughed together and Seth sat beside her towelling the excess water from his hair.

"Excuse me," a deep voice close by called out.

Seth pulled the beach towel down from his face to see a man in a dark business suit standing before him. He was puzzled.

"Me?"

"Yes. Are you Seth Tawnya Jarvis from Hakea Hollow Farm near Cranbrook?"

"Yes. I am."

The man pulled an envelope out of his inside jacket pocket and passed it to Seth.

"Well, consider yourself **served**," he stated in a loud voice. "Sign here to acknowledge that you've received these documents."

Everyone within close vicinity was drawn to the episode unfolding before them. It was a bit hard for the women to ignore. Seth was embarrassed. The suited man turned on his heel and walked away. Seth had no intention of discovering what the contents of the buff-coloured envelope held while he was in such a public place. He put it into the carry bag.

"What is it, Dad? What did that man give you?"

Alicia jumped up to look in the bag, her inquisitive nature prompting her to find out what was going on.

"Not now, Alicia." Seth's cross voice made her withdraw, she knew that tone could not be breached. "Go and play 'Marco Polo' with the other kids, we'll be going soon."

"Already?" she whined. "I thought we were staying." Alicia got a look to match the earlier reaction. "Yes, Dad."

Annie wasn't sure what to make of the whole thing but was aware of Seth's agitation. She didn't know much about the man after only meeting him the day before. But ... she had to ask.

"Are you okay?"

"I think so ..." he said quietly. "I don't know what it's for but I guess I'll find out soon enough."

Annie nodded and left it alone. It wasn't any of her business anyway.

CHAPTER 3

Ryan and Alicia ate their picnic lunch on the verandah outside the guest room. They had their games, colouring books and pencils. Seth told them to leave him alone for a while. Ryan was worried, so Alicia decided it was her job to distract him. Dad had already been cross with her earlier, and he'd told them to stay where they were. He would be back soon.

Seth walked up and down the footpath outside the front of the house in Lancaster Street. He wanted to go for a long walk by himself. Could he leave the children unattended? They were busy and he knew they'd stay there until he came back. He couldn't. It just wasn't right. His unusual behaviour caught the attention of both Liam and his neighbour, Millie.

"Courtney, come into the lounge room," Liam bade his wife. "Take a look at this."

They watched Seth for a bit.

"What's he doing? Is he all right?" Courtney asked Liam.

"Something's up, I think." Liam shrugged and decided to leave it be.

Millie noticed the tall man wearing the Akubra striding back and forth and was reminded of when she'd first seen him a couple of weeks ago. There was still something familiar about him but he was acting a bit odd out there on the path at the moment.

Seth gave up, frustrated, and returned to the children. He would put his jumbled thoughts aside until later.

Dinner was friendly enough. Seth put on a cheerful face but the underlying distraction was evident to his hosts. Fortunately, the kids didn't notice. They went through their usual routine, read bedtime stories and fell asleep.

Seth had the envelope on the bed but didn't pick it up. *Surely not, it couldn't be.* He couldn't lose hope. He looked at it again. *No. I can't open it, not yet.*

Heat rose to his face, his breath caught, and he shook his head. It will have to wait. He paced around the bedroom. His eyes kept wandering back to that wretched envelope sitting there by itself on the bed. It appeared almost animated and that irritated him no end. Seth decided to put it away and have a warm shower. He retired early but wrestled with disturbing dreams and slept little. At first light, he sat outside in the fresh air and prayed for over an hour. An element of peace returned.

He had to face it, no matter what the outcome might be. He tiptoed past his sleeping children and withdrew the envelope. The contents held a sealed Application for Divorce, an Affidavit and a certified copy of his Marriage Certificate. Instructions were provided in a letter with a return address for a lawyer in Perth. Seth exhaled with force. He had dreaded this day; reconciliation wasn't on the agenda, he'd prayed for it, longed for it and wanted his kids to have their Mum back. It wasn't going to happen and he had to accept it. *It's not what I want, Lord. Why does it have to be like this? I don't understand. Maybe* ... he considered the legal documents for a moment before replacing them in the envelope. *I can't sign those forms, not yet.* No, he would have to deal with it another day.

"Okay, today after swimming lessons we're going to visit Auntie Beryl and Uncle Bob," Seth announced. He noticed the look on his daughter's face with dismay.

"But, Dad, it's so boring ..."

"Leesh! That's enough of that. We'll go to the newsagents first and you can both buy a new comic."

Their faces lit up at that suggestion.

"I don't mind going, Dad."

Ryan looked at his father with an earnest expression.

"I know, Ry. Thanks for that, I need to have a chat with Uncle Bob."

"Why do we call them Uncle and Auntie when they aren't our real family, Dad?" Alicia queried.

"Because these people are special to me. Don't forget how much they've helped us. Perhaps you can't remember Alicia. You were probably too little."

"I remember, Dad," Ryan spoke as a matter-of-fact. "And Auntie Jessica, too. She's part of our family."

Seth brushed his hand over his son's hair.

"I know that, Ryan. She's Dad's sister like I'm your sister." Alicia put in knowingly.

"That's right, Leesh. Come on, get your things and let's go."

Swimming lessons went quickly, Bronte and Alicia didn't want to part company and Ryan had enjoyed a good time with Jimmy and Jon. Annie invited them to share a picnic at the pool the next day. Tom had the day off and would be joining them. They would bring the food and drinks for everyone. The children were pleased when Seth agreed.

After eating a pie and sauce for lunch, the trio went to the newsagents in the main street. The kids were surprised when their Dad bought a Phantom comic for himself. With faces smiling, they left for the Webbers.

Alicia wanted to knock on the door. Seth held her up to lift the big black door knocker while she banged it down three times. A smile spread across her face pleasing her father. The door opened.

"Seth. Alicia and Ryan! Come in, come in. Bob's in his office."

Beryl held out her arms to hug them one at a time.

"B-ob," she called out.

The older man came through the door with a huge smile adorning his wise face.

"Hello, Jarvo, how nice. To what do we owe this visit today?" he asked cordially.

Alicia's lips pursed into a hard line, and she breathed out through her nose, annoyed at the nickname again. There was a lengthy pause. Seth turned his new Akubra by its stiff brim round and round in his hands. Bob noticed the nervous action.

"I need to have a chat."

Seth's flat tone disturbed the Reverend, who glanced at his wife with a slight nod of his head.

"Let's go and see the kittens out on the back verandah." Beryl herded the excited children outside with a look over her shoulder. "We'll put the kettle on in a little while."

"Aw, they're so cute. Look, Ry, this one's got pretty grey stripes."

"They've got blue eyes, too. Not green ones like mine," Ryan noticed.

Bob ushered Seth into his study. It's familiarity, with Bob's big desk and books everywhere, was a source of comfort to Seth.

"I've missed you. We haven't seen each other for a while."

"Not since we were at the Stirlings in October. And then only briefly when I dropped the kids off here while I was away during harvest before Christmas."

"What's up, Seth?"

The younger man could hear the children's muffled voices outside. He listened for a few minutes before responding. Bob waited for him to answer when he was ready.

"Do they have names, Auntie Beryl?" Ryan asked.

"Not yet. What do you think the kittens should be called?"

"Maybe Tiger," Alicia looked a bit baffled, "and that one could be Bluey I 'spose. What about the others? They need to have names too."

"How about Smokey and Bandit. Like in the name of the film 'Smokey and the Bandit'; you could have Shadow or Storm or Misty," Beryl suggested. The children sat mesmerised by the antics of the five grey kittens in their box lined with a fluffy towel. Auntie Beryl explained how to pat them gently at first and then she carefully lifted one each onto the children's laps. They were content with the distraction and Seth felt comfortable to begin talking.

"Bob, I got served with a Divorce Application yesterday."

Seth spoke with an edge to his voice. Emotion beginning to surface.

"Oh, Seth. I'm sorry to hear that."

"I wasn't expecting it, and especially not at the swimming pool."

He sighed.

"I wonder how they found you there?"

"Probably went to the farm; could've seen old Fred. He knew we were coming to Mt Barker for swimming lessons. The people at the store in town knew as well. They're holding my mail for me to collect on Saturday."

Another silent pause. Seth felt heat sting at the back of his eyes and nose. He inhaled a ragged breath and put his head in his hands.

"It's not right, Bob."

He wiped moisture away from his eyes.

"I know that's how you feel, son, but if that's what Felicity wants there's not much else you can do."

The men discussed what the procedures might involve. Bob suggested finding a solicitor to handle the details because it would be too hard on Seth to do it himself. They spent some time praying together. The back door banged closed and Bob could hear Beryl in the kitchen getting afternoon tea ready.

"I'll give you a few minutes to yourself. You know where the bathroom is, come out when you're ready."

"Thanks, Bob."

He dug a handkerchief out of his pocket and blew his nose. Seth stood at the window and watched his children. They were so innocent and happy at the moment and he didn't want that spoiled. Ryan had already been affected by his mother leaving. His heart was heavy with the import of what the future would hold for them. He turned and noticed Bob and Beryl's family portrait taken some years ago with their adult son and daughters. How blessed they were.

His eyes strayed to the intricate pencil sketches of native orchids Bob had spent hours drawing from the macro photographs he'd taken for him. Memories of their walks together in the Stirling Ranges flooded his thoughts. They were valued times of sharing, and Bob's wisdom helped him to get through those tough months after Felicity left.

I'd better clean myself up and join the others.

"Dad, you have to come and see the kittens. We've given them names. Pearl, Shadow, Smokey and Bandit. There's one we called Tiger. Can we take it home with us?"

"I knew that was coming. And, no, we can't."

"But ..."

"Sorry, kids, Mallee would chase the cat and cause all sorts of disruption."

That's all I need, another thing to deal with. No thanks.

"Be careful about how much you eat, remember Courtney will have dinner ready for us in a little while."

"You're staying at Lancaster Guest House?" Beryl smiled. "That's much better than running to and from the farm every day."

"It's working well. Do you know Courtney and Liam?"

Seth wasn't aware they knew about the guest house.

"Yes, lovely couple. Got a bit of history there too," Beryl waggled her greying eyebrows. The kids laughed at that.

"Do that again Auntie Beryl, go on, please."

She did, and more giggles ensued.

Beryl slipped Seth an invitation to Bob's surprise 70th birthday party on Saturday week. She pressed a finger to her mouth as a signal not to comment about it in her husband's presence. Seth nodded and smiled.

Three bodies lay across the queen size bed, each held up a comic, reading silently.

"Dad … it wasn't boring this afternoon."

Alicia needed to clear her guilty conscience.

"That's good."

They snuggled closer to each other, and before long, two children were sound asleep. Seth lifted them off his bed and put them in their own.

"Is that coffee I smell in here?"

Seth poked his head around the kitchen door and was welcomed by Liam and Courtney to join them.

"I believe you know good friends of mine."

Seth hesitated when he realised the conversation could get personal. He stirred sugar into his cup.

"Oh, who's that?" Liam put in.

"Beryl and Bob Webber."

"Ah, yes. Reverend Bob and his lovely wife."

Courtney explained how she had come to live in Mt Barker last year, and about the Sydney lawyer finding her to pass on the inheritance from her great uncle.

"I had no idea how important it is to have meaningful relationships," Courtney added. "That's something I've learned since being here."

The trials of growing up as a ward-of-the-state in New South Wales with no family connections or genuine love had made her keep her distance from people. A bad experience in the Children's Home had affected her deeply. Liam followed on with his part of the story and how Reverend Bob had helped them sort through their situation.

"And, here we are, Mr and Mrs Wilson living in Mt Barker, Western Australia and running Lancaster Guest House."

Seth felt comfortable in their company and appreciated the adult conversation.

"I got an invitation to Bob's surprise birthday party ..."

Courtney interrupted him.

"We're going too. I think Beryl has asked the whole nation."

They smiled at her comment.

"Would it be all right for us to stay here on Friday night? It's another day more than I booked in for originally."

Seth would prefer to stay in town and go home on Saturday after the party.

"Not a problem, we'll be glad to have you."

Liam had found a new friend in Seth.

CHAPTER 4

T hursday broke bright and clear. A lovely summer's day and perfect for a picnic. Annie introduced Tom to Seth. He was surprised to find that Tom wasn't quite what he expected. His rough-looks contrasted significantly to Annie's neatness and refinement. He could see that Bronte's red hair came from her father. Tom's long, thin greying hair had streaks of faded auburn through it and his chin wore a sparse red beard. Tom wore a broad-brimmed hat, was slathered with sunscreen and had white zinc on his lips. It wasn't a particularly good look but a necessary one. The men chatted easily and enjoyed having male company amid the mums and kids around the pool. Seth noticed an exposed portion of a tattoo showing under Tom's rolled up shirtsleeve. All he could see was part of a circle and rectangle. He wondered what the tattoo might represent but was too polite to ask, after all, he'd only just met the man. The couple's devotion to each other was obvious from the eye contact and gentle touches they shared.

The twins were climbing the fence by hooking their fingers and toes into the cyclone wire and scaling the high enclosure. Annie passed a concerned glance toward her husband. Tom noticed and understood immediately. No verbal communication was necessary.

"Oh, no. 'Scuse me, I'd better go sort 'em out before the manager gets onto 'em."

Tom rolled his eyes and threw his hands up in the air. Kaimarie was unsettled and needed attention while Annie attempted to put the abundant picnic food out on the rug. The baby's face was flushed. Annie removed the matinee jacket and booties, leaving her in a singlet and frilly pink pilchers over the cloth nappy. Seth offered to take the baby.

"Hello, Kaimarie." He chatted to her in gobbledegook and the child quieted. "So, you just wanted someone to talk to you, didn't you?"

"Dad, you're silly,"

Alicia hadn't seen her father act like this before.

"No different to how I used to talk to you."

He smiled at his daughter. Had it been more than six years since she was born? So much water under the bridge since then. He sighed.

Annie took Kaimarie to give her a bottle of milk. Seth and Tom ate with the five children enjoying fresh sandwiches, cake and watermelon. The baby was passed to Tom for burping while Annie ate her lunch. Kaimarie was content to be passed around and Seth willingly took her again while Tom went to put the rubbish in the bin. The baby was propped up against his shoulder and she soon nodded off to sleep. Annie poured coffee from a thermos into cups for each of them.

"Sugar, Seth?"

"Just the two, please."

Annie chuckled at his comment and shook her head.

"She'll sleep for a while now." Annie placed the little one back in the bassinet. "You're good with kids."

"I had to learn fast, but I must say that was the easy bit."

Seth looked away. Annie thought there was a lot more behind that comment than he was prepared to share.

They returned to Cranbrook straight after swimming lessons on Friday. Seth called in at the shop to collect the mail.

"Jarvo, a fellow came in here looking for you. Said he had something to give to you but wouldn't leave it with us. He looked like an important person. We weren't sure about telling him when he asked where he could find you. We hope it was okay."

"Yeah. He found me. Can you hold my mail again next week, please?"

"Sure."

The couple thought they might get a bit more information about that strange bloke but Seth wasn't explaining anything. They were no wiser than they were before.

Mallee ran out barking a greeting with her tail wagging furiously as soon as they pulled into the driveway.

"You missed us, girl."

Seth patted her. The kids swamped the dog with hugs. She trotted along beside them as they entered the house and then lay down in front of the door when it closed. After unpacking their gear Alicia and Ryan ran outside to ride their bikes and fell into their normal routine.

A picturesque sunset in the west had shimmered with pink and gold wispy clouds, and darkness began to fall. It was quiet in the house, which seemed huge after spending the last few days in one room.

Home. Where the heart was supposed to be, where love and joy and peace should reign. Family growing together with an unbreakable bond. Hakea Hollow Farm had never been the same after 'that' day. Divorce papers were spread out on the table, and Seth held a black biro in his right hand twirling it back and forth. The pen fell and clattered on the tiled floor. Seth's head hung low, he breathed out slowly, his hand rubbed across his face. Memories of Felicity leaving flooded his mind. It felt like yesterday.

Four shearers bent over the ewes with wide combs buzzing through quality fine wool fleeces. Sweat dripped from their noses, foreheads and chins. Strong arms pushed the animals aside and pulled another from the holding pen. Seth had spent the morning with Mallee chasing sheep into the race and up the ramp to the shearing shed. A rousie swept the floor, and the woolclasser checked the clip before it was pressed into the bale. Seth turned the urn on the bench up to high to bring it to the boil. It was nearly time to collect the food for smoko from the house.

The back screen door flew open as Seth, in his sweat-soaked khaki shirt, came into the laundry. He tossed his hat on the washing machine. He stank of sheep and lanolin grease.

"Fliss ... I'm here. I'll just wash up first."

He turned on the tap, soaped up his hands and washed his bristly face. He doused his hair with cold water and dried off on an old towel.

The small old-fashioned kitchen was devoid of any action. No sandwiches, cake or biscuits in containers ready to be picked up and run out to the shed. No bottles of cold water or milk jugs. No Felicity.

"Where are you, hon?"

Panic began to rise in his chest. Was she sick? Had she fallen over? He raced through the house. The bedroom and the bathroom were empty. It was quiet and she was no-where to be found. Seth went toward the front door, maybe she was out in the garden and forgot what the time was. In the passageway he saw an envelope propped up in front of the telephone. His name was written on it in her neat, cursive handwriting. He picked it up, turned it over and opened it. After reading the two-page missive he went weak at the knees. His head swam. He needed to sit down and managed to make it back to the table. She was gone and not coming back.

That was more than two years ago. The farmer looked across at the same kitchen while he was sitting at the same table. Nothing had changed and it still felt empty. Seth wiped his eyes and remembered the rush to procure something for the shearing team to have for morning tea. He had to cook lunch, make afternoon tea then collect Alicia from Kindy and Ryan from school. Do all the things Felicity usually did. Had he taken her for granted? He didn't think so, but the leaden feeling from those words in that letter still sat weighty in the pit of his stomach. It wasn't that simple.

The phone rang. He shook his head to rid himself of the memories and picked up the phone, three pips sounded. He thought it was Jessica.

"Seth, it's me."

It was a familiar female voice, but not his sister.

"Fliss?"

"It's Felicity. You can't call me that anymore. I want to know when you're going to get those papers back to my solicitor."

She was cool and calm.

"I've got them here. I've been reading through it just now."

"Good, we're waiting on them. Tomorrow?" she asked, expecting it done at her say so.

"Are you sure we can't work through this? I want to. We can get help, you know. I'm willing to do it."

"No, Seth. It's over. It was over when I left. I told you I wouldn't come back."

"But the kids ..." his emotions were heightened. His voice rose. "I can't believe you won't even make an effort for them. Do you have any idea how much this has affected Ryan?"

"You're a good Dad, Seth. He'll be fine."

"I can't believe you'd say that." His voice was strained and he resisted the urge to cry. "You just walked away and left us. We loved you and needed you."

Silence.

"I still miss you."

Alicia only remembers you on one or two innocuous occasions.

How could you not want to be a part of her life? Or Ryan's?

Seth only thought these things.

"That's all in the past. I've met someone else and Oliver has asked me to marry him. That's what I want, but I need the divorce so I can get on with my life, Seth."

"So, you don't even care ..." he shouted, his clenched fist waving in the air. A light in the passageway caused Seth to look up. Alicia had opened her door and was listening. Her face pale. Seth baulked at his next sentence. He swallowed hard and calmed himself. He needed to get to his daughter.

"Okay, if that's what you want I'll sign it and send it."

"Thank you. Don't forget to send it Registered mail," and Felicity hung up.

Seth inhaled deeply, slowly, and let out his breath in a rush. He shifted his focus.

"Sorry sweetheart. Did I wake you up?"

Obviously, he thought, cross with himself.

"Who was that Daddy?"

Alicia's sleepy eyes and disorientation made him realise she hadn't understood the conversation. Thankfully.

"It's all right. Come on and I'll tuck you in."

She fell straight back to sleep. Seth sat and watched her gentle breathing before he turned the lamp off. It helped to calm him down. He had worked hard to make the children feel safe and happy after Felicity left. His sister, Jessica, had dropped everything to come and help take care of Alicia and Ryan. He was in the middle of shearing, at the time, and the demands of farm work were enormous.

Seth wiped his eyes with the back of his hand. He'd failed as a husband and struggled in his role as a single father. He'd let his family down and guilt consumed him.

CHAPTER 5

Beryl Webber stood in the doorway of St Oswald's[2] stone church building in Cranbrook while she waited for the children from the district to arrive. Her Sunday School lesson was prepared and the activity sheets were ready to be given out. Reverend Bob would take the service afterwards. Cranbrook was in his parish area and services were held at St Oswald's every second week. Beryl took the class an hour before church was due to start. Today they were looking at the parable of the lost sheep.

Seth parked the car to drop the kids off before heading to the Memorial Hall,[3] where the adult Bible classes were held at the same time. Bob would be leading their time in the Word; they were studying Ephesians and were going to look at Chapter 4 this morning. Beryl waved to Seth as he walked down the street.

"Well, don't you look smart today?"

Beryl smiled at the children as they approached. Alicia had a lilac dress with a fashionable dropped waistline, a white Peter Pan collar and short puff sleeves. She had white sandals on her feet. Ryan wore blue jeans with a blue two-toned knit shirt and denim sneakers. Their hair was combed neatly and they both carried a children's Bible.

---

2   St Oswald's Anglican Church
3   Cranbrook Memorial Hall

"Nanna took us shopping when we went to Bunbury. She buys us something special to wear on Christmas Day. We get to pick the clothes we like best. This was my favourite dress. And I helped Ryan choose which shirt to get because he couldn't decide between two of them. I thought the blue one was better than the yellow one and Nanna agreed with me."

Alicia made sure Auntie Beryl knew the details.

"You look pretty as a picture," Beryl smiled at the little girl.

"I don't look like my Mum, 'cos Nanna said so. I saw a picture of her in the photo album. She died when I was little."

Ryan quickly looked at his sister, his mouth dropped open, and then he looked up at Auntie Beryl. Concern at the comment was written all over his face.

"It's all right, Ryan, I'll talk to Daddy later."

The young boy exhaled loudly and nodded.

The congregation stood around after church had finished and chatted for a while. Beryl approached Seth and indicated for him to come aside to talk privately. He was surprised at Alicia's statement.

"I've never told her that," he assured Beryl. "I wonder why she'd think Felicity died?"

"Your mother-in-law wouldn't have said anything like it, surely."

"No, Nanna and Pop still see Felicity but not very often and never when we are visiting. I can't imagine either of them saying such a thing. They've always been close to the kids and supported me."

"What are you going to do?"

Beryl thought the issue was too important to ignore.

"I'll talk to Alicia, and Ryan too. He'll be upset by what she said. Oh boy, happy days!"

Beryl rubbed his arm in sympathy and put her hands together in a prayer-like pose before she walked away. Seth knew his friends would pray for him and the children while he sorted it out.

"Are we going yet?" Ryan asked.

He'd seen Auntie Beryl talk to Dad like she promised.

"Yes, get Alicia, and we'll head home."

Once the children were strapped in with their seat belts and they drove away, Seth asked what they learned about in Sunday School.

"It was about a sheep, Dad." Alicia loved bible stories. "It got lost and the shepherd had to go and find it. It was still alive, not like our lambs that die in the cold weather."

Seth's eyes widened, then his eyebrows gathered together in a frown. Maybe she had an issue with death he didn't know about. Ryan interrupted.

"The whole story was about being happy the lost one was found, Alicia, not about dying sheep."

Seth coughed, then decided it was now or never.

"So, Leesh, Auntie Beryl tells me you think your Mum died. Is that right?"

"Yeah, when I was little, but I don't remember."

"What makes you think she died?"

Seth's hands gripped the steering wheel tighter.

"Well, she went away and never came back like Granny and Grandad."

Oh, so that explains it. Seth caught the look in Ryan's eyes in the rear-view mirror.

"They were old and sick." She continued, "I said goodbye to them, though. Do you remember when we went to the hospital? It wasn't very nice and Granny looked terrible. She said she was ready to meet God and was going to wait for me to come and join her one day. Then Grandad did the same. He went to heaven, too."

They pulled into the driveway and parked the car in the garage.

"Come with me, both of you."

Seth took them to the lounge room and sat Alicia on his knee. Ryan sat beside his father.

"Leesh, you need to know that your Mum didn't die like you think she did."

Ryan shook his head. Alicia looked at him and back to her Dad.

"But, does that mean ..." confused at what they were saying, she stopped mid-sentence.

"Yes, Alicia, your Mum is still alive."

Tears filled Ryan's eyes. He reached out for his little sister's hand and held it.

"Why doesn't she live with us? Other kids Mum's live at home with them."

Seth's heart was burdened. What was the right thing to say? He didn't want to hurt her.

"Your Mum decided to live somewhere else, Leesh."

"Why?"

"It's complicated, honey."

How are you supposed to explain abandonment to a six-year-old?

"Okay, maybe I'll understand it better when I grow up some more."

She hopped off and went outside to throw the ball for Mallee.

Was it really that simple? Seth was surprised. She was so accepting but he'd better watch her. He knew she would process it and be back with more questions. Ryan sat still. Tears ran down his young cheeks. He sniffed.

"Oh, Ry, come here."

The eight-year-old boy hopped onto his Dad's lap and had a cuddle.

"I don't get it, Dad. I'm glad we've got you."

That did Seth in; he shed a tear too.

Courtney was looking for the Telecom bill. She was sure it had come last week, and it was due to be paid by Tuesday.

"Liam, do you know where that phone bill is? I can't find it anywhere."

"I think I put it in the drawer of my beside table. I didn't want to leave it laying around when we had guests coming into the house for dinner," he answered.

Courtney headed down the passageway to their bedroom. She quickly pulled out the drawer, and in her haste it fell off the rails and dropped onto the floor.

"Oh, bother."

Courtney took the bill off the top and put it on the bed. Then bent to pick up the contents and return them to the drawer. A yellowed newspaper article caught her eye. She noticed the headline '4 Killed in Plane Crash'. The clipping was dated 22 July, 1966 and showed a photograph of the crumpled wreckage. The article explained it: the private twin-engine Piper Comanche charter aeroplane was to fly three mining business passengers from Mt Isa to Brisbane. Shortly after becoming airborne, the left engine failed. The pilot applied full right rudder to counter the yaw and banked to counter adverse roll. It maintained directional control but because the landing gear wasn't retracted, and the pilot failed to lower the nose of the aircraft to compensate for the loss of power, it stalled and crashed.

The report listed the names of the deceased: Mr James Johnson, 43, pilot from Brisbane, Queensland; Mr Richard Lawrence, 30, passenger from Sydney, New South Wales; Mr Michael Lancaster, 28, and his wife, Mrs Claire Lancaster, 27, passengers from Perth, Western Australia.

Courtney re-read the list. Her parents! Her parents were in that terrible accident. She'd never known how they died. Courtney's strength weakened and she had to sit down on the bed. Her lips trembled and her heart filled with a dire heaviness. My poor Mum and Dad, this is awful. Courtney sat stunned for some time staring vacantly at the wall. Uncle Geoff must have kept the clipping since it happened. She wondered why she hadn't seen it before when she'd used that drawer.

"Liam?" her voice broke as she called out to him from the bedroom.

"Yeah," he came to the door and stopped. His face blanched. "Oh, you've found the article."

His voice was strained. Her head lifted and a flicker of anger stirred in her eyes.

"You knew. You knew this was in here?"

"Yes."

"How long?"

"After Christmas when we were packing up. It fell out of one of Uncle Geoff's diaries."

"What? I don't believe it. You've had this for over two weeks and didn't show me?"

Courtney raised her voice in disbelief.

"I'm sorry, Courtney. I was trying to figure out when would be the right time. I knew it would be upsetting, and I confess I'd forgotten about it with the busyness of guests in the house."

She stood and slammed the drawer closed. The article still in her hand. Courtney picked up the Telecom bill and shoved it at Liam.

"Of course I would be upset. Didn't it occur to you that I had a right to know?"

She walked around to her side of the bed and sat with her back to him.

"Go away and leave me alone. I don't want to talk to you."

It wasn't long before he heard her sobs. All he wanted to do was take her in his arms and hold her. Liam felt remorse engulf him. He should have done something about it after New Year's Day but he kept putting it off. He'd give her the space she needed, but he had a feeling they were facing their first serious tiff since they'd been living as man and wife.

CHAPTER 6

C landestine meetings, covert arrangements and conspiring whispers were wearing Beryl down. She would never organise a surprise party again. It was too taxing having to watch what she said to Bob without slipping up or telling him lies. Saturday couldn't come soon enough.

The Ladies' Bible Study group were helping cater for the afternoon tea. Lamingtons, slices and cakes were in the freezer; sausage rolls would be cooked on the day, and fresh sandwiches were going to be put together just before the event.

Beryl was booked into the hairdresser's for a perm on Wednesday. She didn't have time to waste, but the thought of just sitting and flipping through a Woman's Day magazine held a lot of appeal for her. *I'll be able to catch my breath,* she thought, as she hung out her Monday morning load of washing.

The sight of the signed document on the dash seared into the corner of Seth's eye as he drove from the farm to Mt Barker. They'd left home early to get to the post office before swimming lessons started. That envelope felt like a hot potato in his hands and he had to get rid of it. The knowledge of what it contained burned right through him. 'Irreconcilable differences' ran through his mind. He didn't agree. In his opinion it could and should be worked out, but it was quite clear that Felicity had no intention of making it happen. The whole issue sat heavy on his heart. He told the kids to wait in the car with the windows down while he dashed into the building.

"Registered mail, please."

He handed the envelope over the counter to the clerk, signed it and paid the fee. Relieved it was done, he strode outdoors to the car to get on with his day.

How am I supposed to put that behind me and not worry about it? I guess it will make Felicity happy, probably the best thing I've ever done in her opinion. I mustn't think like that. I have to stop those thoughts from getting in. But a root of bitterness had taken a tentative hold.

The atmosphere at the swimming pool lightened his mood. The smell of chlorine, whistles blowing and teachers with happy children splashing and smiling rubbed off on him. He needed to relax and enjoy the time with Alicia and Ryan. It didn't take long to find their new friends. Annie welcomed them back with a warm smile and a wave to indicate they had saved a spot for them to sit together.

"How was your weekend, Seth?"

"Um," he hesitated unsure of how he should respond.

Annie's gaze deepened. It wasn't going to be a generic answer. Perhaps she had asked a more poignant question than she realised.

"Not the best."

"I'm sorry to hear that. Are you okay?"

Maybe she shouldn't have asked that either.

"I hope so. It's been a hard couple of days. I'm the one who is sorry, Annie."

He wanted to back off but felt the burden too big. Sharing with a 'stranger' might be easier than saying anything to someone close to him.

"I had to post off divorce papers this morning."

There, he got it out. He had to face the fact that he would soon be a divorced man.

"Oh," she paused, "I thought your wife must have been at work or was sick."

Seth shook his head.

"Was that something to do with those papers last week?"

"Yeah. Not what I want but it's out of my hands."

"Such a shame."

Compassion filled her quiet words.

"I know, but I have to trust it will work itself out. In the long run, that is."

"Can I pray for you?" Annie offered.

Seth took a second look at the woman across from him.

"You're a Christian?" She nodded in response. "I should've figured that out before. I'd appreciate your prayers, thanks."

The pair sat in silence for a while, contemplating their discussion. A peace washed over Seth and he felt at ease with the new friend and confidant God had led him to. He'd pretty much isolated himself from most people over the past two years. Apart from the lack of time, he hadn't wanted to share his feelings with anyone other than Bob.

The shrill sound of a whistle blew to indicate the end of another swimming class. The girls came back with their beach towels slung across their shoulders.

"Dad, can we go to Bronte's house for a visit?"

Alicia asked within earshot of Annie.

"It's manners to wait until you're invited."

Sometimes Seth was embarrassed by his daughter's forward nature. It was so unlike his own.

"You might like to come home with us after lessons one day and stay for a sleepover. Would you like to do that?"

Alicia's grin was wide, her eyes danced.

"Can I, pleeease, Dad?"

"Ryan can come too," Annie added.

"Go on, Dad, let us do it."

She fluttered her eyelashes at him. Seth couldn't help but smile.

"You are a ratbag, do you know that Alicia Sasha Jarvis?" He shook his head and grimaced but not out of ire. "I'll think about it and we will have a discussion, little Miss."

"Okay, Dad."

Even at six-years-old, Alicia knew when not to push too hard.

Annie was pensive a moment before speaking up.

"Sasha, you said. Didn't that man last week say a Russian-sounding middle name for you?"

"Yes. Mine is Tawnya. It means 'a green field' and I think my mother thought it would be a good name for a farmer's son. She had a Russian heritage. My great, great, great-grandfather jumped ship in about 1830 with some other sailors. They saw Australia as the land of opportunity and took it. That's all I know, Mum had an old daguerreotype photo of him that was taken in 1842 at a portrait studio in Sydney. She told us stories she heard from her grandmother when she was a child." He paused, and then continued.

"It's all a bit vague, really, but that's how we ended up with those names. My sister's name is Jessica Tatiana, and Mum was called Ana – for Anastasia; I didn't realise that until I was twelve-years-old when Jess was born. I should be grateful they weren't our given names. Imagine, light green eyes and a name like Tawnya. We do affectionately call each other 'Tawny' and 'Tati' at times. Just as well there was only two of us."

He chuckled and shrugged his shoulders.

"There's twelve years between you and your sister. That's a big gap."

"Change of life baby, I believe." Seth raised his eyebrows. "I didn't want to know about it at the time, but she was a good baby. I enjoyed having a little sister, and helped to spoil her, too. I wouldn't want to be without her now."

He smiled at the memories of watching her grow through her baby stages. And the joy of sharing his life with a little girl who became the wonderful young woman she is now. Seth decided to keep the tradition of Russian names for Alicia to please his mother. It brought to mind the meaning of Sasha that he'd chosen for her. It meant defender, helper of mankind. That made sense given her nature and how she looked out for her older brother and protected him. Almost fiercely, at times. Ryan was named after his grandfather. 'Ryan William Jarvis' which had thrilled Seth's dad when he'd learned of it.

His thoughts had wandered quite a bit when he realised Annie was waving goodbye and he hadn't noticed the family pack up to leave. He waved in return and then shuttled his kids off to the showers before they went to find a cafe for some lunch.

Liam was on the front verandah when they arrived back at the guest house.

"Want to join me?" he called to Seth, holding up a cold can.

"I don't drink beer very often, but you know what, today I will. I'll get the kids sorted out and then come back."

Liam got up and went to the fridge to get another beer for their guest. He rarely drank alcohol himself but today he was enjoying it. When Seth came up the steps, he passed him the drink.

"Thanks."

He pulled the ring back and the gas released with a fizzing sound. A yeasty scent wafted under his nose as he tipped it up and took a mouthful. He blew out a deep breath.

"Not such a good day for you either?" Liam queried.

"Woman problems, I guess you could say."

"You, too. I'm being served hot tongue and cold shoulder at the moment."

Liam plastered a supercilious smile on his face. He wasn't too perturbed. Not that he was being blasé about the situation, he just wanted a release from the tension. He was giving his wife time to deal with the issue.

"I inadvertently neglected to tell Courtney about finding a newspaper article with details of the aircraft accident her parents had died in."

His voice was soft and sad. Seth was surprised. He didn't know anything about these people. Liam explained the situation and they spoke for over an hour out there together. They heard voices inside the house.

"Nearly dinner time." Liam's eyes twinkled. "I hope we get different food on the menu tonight."

Courtney was much more relaxed with helping the children to set the table while she listened to Alicia's chatter. Ryan was warming to her and began to include himself in the conversation. The hostess couldn't hold onto the unforgiving resistance she'd held against Liam. He noticed her softening attitude straight away when they walked into the kitchen. Relief and compassion flooded through him. She was right. He should have told her he'd found it and prepared her to receive the news. He sidled up beside her.

"Sorry, honey."

His whispered apology was acknowledged with a nod of her head.

"The food's ready to be put on the table," Courtney announced.

Everyone took their familiar places and sat down.

"Ryan, would you say grace for us tonight?" Liam asked.

The boy glanced at his Dad, who sent an encouraging look for him to oblige.

"Yeah. Okay, I will."

Seth beamed at his son. This visit had more benefits than he'd anticipated. They closed their eyes.

"Dear Lord Jesus, thank you for this food that Courtney made. It's delicious, much better than Dad's cooking. And thanks for our new friends. Amen."

It took all the adults' effort not to burst out laughing. Courtney was especially touched by his words. Her heart melted. *What a precious little boy*, she thought.

The surprise 70th birthday party was on at 2.00pm. Seth and Beryl had colluded to get Bob away from the manse and church building by arranging a visit to Liam's after lunch. Beryl's pre-arranged signal to let everyone know Bob had left home was to be two rings of the phone and then she'd hang up. That way she couldn't get caught up in unnecessary conversations. Millie's phone rang twice and stopped, as did Courtney's. Bob was on his way.

Courtney and Liam quickly made a trip to take the tray of cream lamingtons from the fridge, along with plates of sandwiches covered with plastic wrap through the back gate to Millie's place. They loaded up the car and waited in the driveway.

When Bob's white Toyota Corolla with a gold pin-stripe parked beside the kerb out the front of Lancaster Guest House, Millie's little mustard-coloured Datsun 120Y pulled away. The women waved to Bob as they passed by.

"Do you think he suspects anything, Millie?"

Courtney hoped this could be pulled off after Beryl's nerve-racking weeks of waiting for today. So much planning needed a positive outcome for her.

"He has no idea," Millie laughed. "No idea, whatsoever."

CHAPTER 7

Tables covered in hand-embroidered cloths with small vases of home-grown flowers were dotted around the lawn near the bell tower. Fortunately, it was a calm afternoon where only a gentle breeze played with the corners of the tablecloths. Plates and serviettes were on a trestle under the shade of a tree. A seemingly synchronised arrival of cars pulled into the church car park with passengers alighting bearing food-laden platters.

Mavis needed help to carry the large fruit cake she'd made for the celebratory birthday to the cake table. Adorned in bright white royal icing with a neat scalloped edge, a "Happy 70th Birthday, Bob" message was piped around exquisite hand-sculptured native spider orchids set in the centre. Everyone was pleased with the impressive job Mavis had done. Beryl decided it was too hard to try and light candles outdoors and Mavis agreed. They could sing Happy Birthday and give three cheers and that would be enough.

Family and friends started to arrive at two o'clock, and Beryl began to fret that the men distracting Bob might forget to make sure he got back soon. Fifteen minutes later she saw his car drive in slowly. Bob's face was a puzzle – he thought he'd forgotten a significant event on his church calendar.

"Surprise!"

"What have I missed? Who's the surprise for?"

Bob was concerned until Beryl came forward with a glowing smile at achieving her goal.

"Happy Birthday, dear."

The crowd burst into song, cheers rang out, and Bob was genuinely moved by the thoughtfulness. He'd even forgotten it was his birthday!

"How did you do this?" He shook his head. "Thanks love," and he gave her a big kiss in front of everyone. More cheers and hoots followed, and a bounty of food and drinks were passed around.

Millie took plates piled with sausage rolls and bowls of tomato sauce to put on the small tables where guests gathered around them. The aroma from the baked puff-pastry enticed everyone to enjoy the savouries while they were still hot. The last table Millie served was near the car park where Courtney and Liam sat.

"Millie, come and have a cuppa and something to eat," Courtney invited. "You've been running around for ages. It's time you stopped for a break."

"You're right, and I will. I forget I'm not as young as I used to be."

Liam stood and gave his chair to her. He sat on his haunches beside her. A red ute roared to a halt and parked under the shade of a nearby tree. Todd got out to join the party. He'd been on an urgent job at a building site out of town and was later than he'd anticipated.

"Whoa, look at you!" Courtney commented.

A smile broke across Todd's face.

"Man, you look different. If I hadn't seen you get out of your car, I wouldn't have known it was you."

Liam rose and gave him a friendly slap on the back. The long-haired surfie image was gone. A neat haircut with a short flick-back fringe framed the handsome face showing off azure blue eyes and perfect white teeth. Jeans and a button-through shirt replaced the usual board shorts and singlet style he'd worn for years.

"Who is she?" Liam wanted to know, asking with an exaggerated wink.

"No-one special. I thought it was time for a change."

Todd responded pleasantly to the probe with a cheeky grin.

"Are you sure about that?" Liam wasn't convinced. "Wink, wink, nudge, nudge."

Liam elbowed him in the ribs, his eyebrows lifting in quick succession.

"Well, you've certainly achieved a dashing clean-cut image, Todd. You look great," Millie added.

Todd helped himself to a generous serving of sausage rolls and tomato sauce.

"Your appetite's still the same." Courtney shook her head in disbelief.

"Didn't have time for lunch. I'm hungry."

He added a few sandwiches and cakes to his plate and ate voraciously. The conversation stalled while they watched him devour it all.

Seth had been talking to Beryl and Bob to wish him a Happy Birthday when Alicia came running up to her father and attempted to pull him away.

"Hang on a minute," he admonished. "I'll be right with you."

Ryan had been standing beside him waiting quietly until he saw the twins. He ran to join them. Seth excused himself and turned his attention to his daughter.

"Daddy, I had a great time at Bronte's. She's got a pretty pink bedroom and I want one, too. Can I?"

She didn't wait for his answer and continued with enthusiasm.

"It was fun helping with the baby. I wish we had one."

Seth was left shaking his head at that comment but before he could say anything she was off again telling him more about her visit at the O'Reilly's.

"We played in a special wooden cubby house. It's got a stove, and a table and chairs and plates and cups, and everything. And Bronte's got a Cabbage Patch doll and we changed its clothes, and ... "

A sound distracted her, Ryan called out when he fell over and skinned his knee. Seth strode over and bent down to check on him. Alicia followed - worried about her brother.

"You're okay, Ry." He brushed the dirt off the superficial graze. "It's not serious."

Courtney had watched the incident as it played out in front of her.

"Seth, we've got a first aid kit in the car if you want it," she offered.

"It's not bleeding. I think I'll just clean it with some water for now."

Seth stood. He didn't know the people at Liam and Courtney's table.

"Seth, this is our friend Todd York."

He removed his hat and put out his hand.

"Hello, Todd, nice to meet you."

Todd shook the offered hand and smiled. He was struck by the familiarity of the eyes that locked with his. Memories pulsed through him.

"Hi."

He pushed out the word and waited with nervous anticipation. Courtney turned to introduce the older woman.

"This is our neighbour, Millie Lockridge. Oh, and she's our friend too." She added this with a grin.

Seth looked around to reach across and greet her as well. Millie's breath caught in her throat and she began to cough. Her face paled, she felt lightheaded, and darkness closed in on her. Millie went to take hold of the table, but it was too late, she fainted.

"Oh, no. Millie." Courtney stood to help the woman slumped over in the chair. "What happened? She must've choked on something. Is she breathing? Liam, what should we do?"

"Todd, help me get her off the chair and lay her down on the grass."

The men kept the concerned guests back to give her plenty of space. Liam checked her airway, it was clear. A few minutes later she came to and looked around unsure of what had happened.

"Millie, it's okay. You fainted, just stay there. We'll help you get up in a little while."

Liam's reassuring tone calmed her.

"Do you want some water, Millie?"

Courtney bit her lip while she patted the back of her friend's hand. Millie nodded. Todd and Liam helped her to a sitting position while Courtney went to the kitchen for a glass of tap water. After a few sips, Millie thought she'd be all right to stand.

"I don't usually get that kind of reaction from people when I meet them," Seth commented, trying to lighten the moment. "I hope you'll be all right."

Millie attempted a half-smile, bewildered, her hands shaky.

"Thanks. I'm sure I'll come good soon."

She noticed the children with him. Seth excused himself and walked away with Alicia in tow to clean the scratch on Ryan's knee. Todd spoke quietly to Liam with a suggestion and then went to open the passenger door of the ute ready for Millie. His mother approached him.

"What's going on, Todd?"

Confusion clouded her mind. Helen was anxious for her long-time friend.

"She fainted, Mum. I'm going to take her home now. Can you get her things and bring the car back to her place when you've finished here?"

His no-nonsense approach matched his new appearance, and Helen decided not to interfere with the arrangement. *Very mature*, she thought, *I'm proud of you, son.*

"Sure, Dad can follow and pick me up from there."

With that sorted out he returned to Millie.

"Come on. I'm taking you home for a rest."

Todd put Millie's arm through his and helped her into the car. Neither said a word on the way there. It wasn't until they sat settled at the kitchen table with the cup of tea Todd insisted on making that he broached the subject that consumed them.

"I know, Millie."

She looked at him and shrugged her shoulders.

"What do you know, or think you know, Todd?"

She was becoming irritated with him. She wanted to be left alone, and he wouldn't leave.

"It's him, isn't it?"

Millie's face blanched.

"You won't faint again, will you?"

He started to get up.

"No."

He sat back down.

Tears pooled in her tired eyes.

"I overheard a conversation you had with Mum when I was about 14, I think." Todd went on. "I wanted something to eat and went to go into the kitchen, but I heard someone crying. I stopped outside the door. It wasn't closed properly and ..."

Millie interrupted him.

"What? What are you saying, Todd?"

"I'm saying that I heard everything. The whole thing, Millie."

She sat in stunned silence. A sick feeling in the pit of her stomach vied to overwhelm her. Elbows rested on the table and her slightly wrinkled hands covered her eyes. She inhaled and released a deep breathy sigh.

"Oh, my goodness. I can't believe it. You've kept that secret all these years."

The young man nodded.

"All these years," she repeated, "and finally, I meet him, like this."

Todd reached across the table and took her hands in his. A gesture that moved the older woman's heart. She had underestimated this boy, or rather, the man he'd become.

"There's no doubt, Millie, even I can see it. He's just like Harold. There's no mistaking those eyes. Or the way he walks, either."

"No, you're right. He is his father's son. Seth, his name is Seth."

CHAPTER 8

Cranbook's school bus pulled up at the farm gate. Alicia clambered down the steps with her Rainbow Brite backpack on and carrying her reading book. Ryan's bag was slung over one shoulder, and the zip on the pocket knocked into the door as he got out. Another flake of orange paint dislodged from the already chipped and worn edge. They ran across to the shelter in the pouring rain, then turned and waved goodbye to Fred.

Hakea Hollow Farm was the last stop on this bus route. The Jarvis kids were the first passengers on in the morning and the last ones to get off in the afternoon. Fred saw Seth driving toward them to collect the children, and was assured they weren't going to be left there for long. It would be a cold wait outside, and he had, on occasion, during winter kept the children on the bus in the warm until their father arrived

He does an incredible job for a bloke on his own. Don't reckon I'd be able to do it, Fred thought as he headed home to his property a few kilometres down the road. He'd been driving the school bus for decades, loved the interaction with the children and watched them grow into fine young men and women. His admiration for Seth grew with each passing year. It had been a happy time when the community witnessed the romance and marriage of the tall farmer and the pretty school teacher. He parked the bus under its shelter and pulled his jumper over his head.

"Fred, where's your raincoat? You'll catch your death out there in this weather."

Fred's wife, Eunice, scolded him.

"I've been expecting you. Sit down, and I'll make us a cuppa, then you can tell me all about today's adventures."

Eunice took great pleasure in hearing the stories about the children and their antics on the bus run. She sometimes went along for the ride herself.

"I was just thinking about Seth and his little kiddies. He's doin' a great job with 'em."

Fred's mind had churned over his earlier thoughts.

"How long ago is it since that slip of a girl came to teach at the school? Can you remember?"

Eunice was surprised at his question and had to do a minor calculation to work it out.

"Well, it must be about ten years. Seth and Felicity were married for about a year before they had Ryan, and he's eight now. It was a match made in heaven, or so we thought at the time."

She pushed her glasses up on her nose and shook her head.

"They were a handsome couple, weren't they? She was a terrific school teacher. The students learned their lessons well in her classroom. I remember Seth was quiet and shy and she drew him out of himself." Eunice paused. "I guess we all pushed them together in the end, hey?"

The locals were thrilled with the idea of the city girl falling in love with the bachelor farmer. They'd encouraged the short romance with a match-making event or two.

"She was a beautiful bride."

Fred smiled at the memory of seeing the way Seth looked at her when she walked down the make-shift aisle on the farm's front lawn.

"Seth just about burst with pride ..."

Eunice interrupted.

"Didn't he just?"

Both went quiet for a few minutes.

"Such a sad ending."

"Not what we expected, that's for sure."

Fred sneezed.

"Bless you."

He took another biscuit from the leafy green Carlton Ware plate.

"So, now, tell me something to brighten my day, dear."

Eunice prompted her husband to dig them out of the gloomy reverie they'd fallen into.

"Did those naughty boys at the back of the bus throw any apple cores out of the window?"

"Not on my watch. They know I'll make them clean the bus on Saturday if they do."

Fred pulled his handkerchief out of his pocket and blew his nose.

"See, now you've got the sniffles. Oh, dear, what am I going to do with you?"

Ryan and Alicia sat at the table with their homework spread out before them. Alicia had been going through her list of words for the spelling bee the next day. Even though she was only in second grade, she was good at spelling and liked to win. The radio was on and Seth was peeling potatoes.

"What's for dinner tonight, Dad?"

Alicia asked the same question every day at the same time.

"Bangers and mash." Seth added, "with gravy."

"Yum. I like it when we get gravy."

Ryan lifted his head from where he was bent over, working on a math problem.

"Me, too. Remember when we stayed at Courtney and Liam's in January? She's such a good cook."

"So, you're not thrilled with my farm-style food? Is that what you're saying, Ry?"

His son didn't see through the tongue-in-cheek question.

"No, Dad, sorry. You cook just fine. I only liked it because of the different stuff we got there."

Seth turned and pulled a funny face. They laughed together. Ryan realised he was only joking and then they pulled more faces at each other.

"And don't do that when you're with other people, either," Seth instructed both of his children.

"Not even at Bronte's?"

Alicia thought the O'Reilly family would understand about face-pulling.

"Oh, well, I guess there might be times when it could be appropriate."

The phone rang. Seth sat the saucepan on the stove and turned the gas on before he went into the hallway. He picked up the receiver.

"Hello, Seth."

It was a long-distance call.

"Fli..," he pulled himself up and tried again. "Felicity?"

"Yes, it's me. Did you get an envelope in the mail today?"

"I did." He added quickly, "I haven't had time to have a look at it yet."

What with bringing in the washing off the back verandah that had taken two days to dry; collecting the kids at pick-up time, and giving them afternoon tea. Helping with homework and getting dinner ready ...like I'm going to rush and open mail I don't want to read.

His thoughts ran away with him, just as well he didn't voice them, that would not have gone down well. He would've sounded like a bitter old housewife.

"The date is set for Wednesday 29th July, in three weeks. You don't have to be in Perth but I think you should come."

He felt prickled by the heat of frustration that rose in his chest, and discomfort at her expectations annoyed him. He did not want to discuss this while the children were within earshot. Talk about 'inappropriate' behaviour. Felicity showed a significant lack of consideration, calling at this time in the afternoon.

"I'll discuss it with my solicitor. He has the details."

Seth wasn't going to talk to her about his plans. He was getting agitated, and this conversation needed to stop before he became angry again. It probably riled him more than it should have. The solicitor had advised Seth to remain calm and allow him to relay any communications between the two parties.

"Well, Oliver and I want this to go ahead without any hiccups."

It was about what she wanted again. And as for Oliver, who the hell was he anyway?

Seth bit his lip.

"Yes, I know. Thanks for ringing."

He hung up which he would've considered rude once, but he was not going to be provoked into an argument. The phone rang. He picked it up and put it straight back down again. Surely Felicity would get the message from that action.

Seth thought it ironical that his divorce was to be addressed in court on the day that Lady Diana Spencer and Prince Charles would be married. It would be the most televised Royal Wedding ever to be held in London. He hoped they would have more success with their marriage than he had experienced.

He made a coffee and took it into the study. The cup sat half-full on a coaster at the corner of his desk. Reluctantly, he picked up the manila envelope that was delivered to the letterbox at the farm gate, and slit it open. He read the documents advising of court dates and court event fees; as well as filing fees and processing information.

Seth slumped back into his swivel desk chair with his elbows on the armrests. He took a breath and slowly released it. He reached across, picked up the documents and shoved them back into the envelope. As he tossed the paperwork aside it caught the handle on the cup and knocked it over.

Coffee spilled over the desk and pooled on the envelope. Seth muttered some long-forgotten swear words he'd not used since being a teenager. It surprised him. Angry with himself, and at his circumstances, he jumped up and grabbed some tissues to mop up the mess. He threw the sodden tissues in the bin and slumped back into his chair again.

His face crumpled. He held his head in his hands and sobbed. Seth's body shook with the emotional pain that had built up over the past weeks. His nervous tension was released. Peace of mind had eluded him for days and God felt far away. Seth wiped his eyes with the back of his hands.

Pick yourself up, dust yourself off, and get on with it. His father's admonishing voice echoed in his head. He had to keep going whether he liked it or not. And not going on would be his preferred option, but he had the kids to take care of and they were solely his responsibility.

CHAPTER 9

The phone rang again. Seth let it ring out, pretending not to notice the annoying trill reverberating in the passage. That was the third time in an hour and he had no intention of answering it. At five o'clock, it rang again.

"I'll get it, Dad." Alicia went to get up from the table but Seth pushed her down with a gentle touch.

"It's all right, Leesh. I'll go."

Panic began to set in but he managed to control it. He most certainly did not want his daughter to answer the phone with her mother on the other end of the line. His finger slid across the hook switch to stop it from ringing, and he bent down to unplug the cord until after the kids went to bed.

"Who was it, Dad?"

Why did Alicia have to be so inquisitive? Ryan never asked those questions. Where does she get that trait from? Maybe it was because she was a girl, girls tended to do that.

"Just a wrong number."

Seth felt uncomfortable lying to her. It did not sit well on his conscience. It hadn't occurred to him until that moment that the caller could be someone other than Felicity. He was going nuts. He was sure of it. *Paranoid is what I've become,* he thought.

He went to the fridge to get some vegetables out for dinner. He noticed Courtney's 21st Birthday dinner invitation for the 11th July. Alicia had put it there with a magnet to remind him to reply by this Friday. They would go and it would be good to catch up with his friends again. Since the summer holidays, they'd attended church at St Oswald's on one Sunday and gone to All Saints Anglican Church in Mt Barker on the alternate week.

It had been a life-line for him. Liam, Todd and Keith had become fast friends. The O'Reilly's had become family friends and they often shared Sunday afternoons together out at the winery. Bob continued to support him with sound advice and friendly chats, but it was great to have the companionship of men closer in age to himself.

He nearly forgot to plug the phone-line back into its socket. It was late when he remembered, and then it rang again. He snatched it up.

"Stop hassling me, Felicity. Talk to my solicitor. This has got to stop," he yelled.

Just before he went to return the handset to its cradle, he heard his sister's voice.

"Seth, wait, it's me."

He felt sick.

"Jess, I'm sorry."

"What is going on? I've been trying to get you for days. Why has Felicity been calling you? You haven't told me anything. Tell me, Seth. I'm not accepting any excuses."

His sharp intake of breath exhaled with a puff and blow.

"She wants a divorce. And she's getting it. Oliver *somebody* wants to marry her."

There was the crux of the matter. He wasn't good enough for her but Oliver was.

"Okay, and I take it you're not travelling too well with all of this."

"Nup, I guess you could say that."

Jessica took in the news that had taken her by surprise. Seth did not usually behave like this. It reminded her of his reaction a couple of years ago.

Jess removed her nurse's cap and put the hair clips in the dish on her dressing table. She'd finished the third evening in a row of night-shift. It was good to be home. She managed to drum up something to eat and enjoyed a cup of tea. While she luxuriated in a long, hot shower the phone rang, she grabbed a towel and wrapped it around herself. A puddle of water gathered on the tiles in the kitchen of her modern flat. She drip-dried while standing there as she spoke to her brother. Seth was a mess. Through the mumbled, panicked and emotional conversation Jessica surmised that Felicity had left.

"I don't know what to do, Jessica. Tell me what I should do, please? I can't think straight and we're in the middle of shearing."

The distress in his plea hit her hard. Seth was always the calm one giving advice, not asking for it.

"Okay," her nursing mode kicked in. "Ring Mum and Dad and let them know what's going on. Take the kids to their place in town and drop them off. Pack spare uniforms and play clothes; don't forget teddies and pyjamas. Oh, and their toothbrushes. Mum can organise school lunches for Ryan and take Leesh to Kindy. They can look after them until I get there."

Her last shift would finish on Friday morning and then she had four days off. The drive down to the farm at Cranbrook would take about three and a half hours. If she slept for a few hours, she'd be okay to travel. She wouldn't have to stop for fuel along the way if she filled up in Perth beforehand, and she could take a thermos of coffee. It would be best to get there as soon as possible. Another thought struck her and she rang Seth back.

"Give Eunice a call, Seth, and ask her if she can cook for the shearers. She'll be able to manage it. Tell her to keep it simple but plenty of it. You can't take care of that and everything else as well. When I get down there, we can sit down and work out a plan for the short term. Okay?"

"Yeah. I should've told you Felicity's note said I couldn't contact her. And she's not coming back. Ever."

It was unbelievable and Jessica couldn't understand what had gone wrong.

"My poor Tawny."

Her heart broke for him, and the instinct to use their pet names struck a chord of compassion that sent a healing balm to her brother.

"Thanks, Tati. I'll see you on Friday night."

Seth whispered a hoarse goodbye and hung up.

Jessica wandered in a daze back to the bathroom and finished drying her hair. She looked at herself in the mirror. Worry lines had developed on her broad forehead that hadn't been there an hour ago. Her brown, almond-shaped eyes set under thick dark brows now reflected pain.

She was a plain woman with typical northern Russian skin, wide mouth and full lips. Her long sculpted nose a feature on her heart-shaped face. When she was growing up, she longed for Seth's tall frame and slimness. She'd always called herself 'chunky' - not fat, but solid, her features inherited from her mother. Her brown hair still had a healthy shine, but her mother's hair had been quite grey. Two peas-in-a-pod, that's what Dad had always called them.

The senior Jarvis' were too elderly to take care of their grandchildren for an extended period. Jess knew the kids' boundless energy and Alicia's nearly four-year-old incessant chatter would wear them down quickly. Two days would be long enough.

Jess had three months long-service leave owing and it looked like the planned trip to Europe would have to go on hold. She'd been going to backpack from Amsterdam in the west to the eastern European countries. Then explore the region their long-ago sea-faring relative had left behind. She would see the Registrar at the hospital tomorrow and make arrangements to take her holiday leave effective from Friday. Her brother needed her, and she would be there for him, no matter what.

It looked like she was going to have to do it again. No holidays available this time though, her mind flitted to the European tour she'd returned from recently. It had been a whirlwind trip, not the planned leisurely one she'd missed out on, but it had been fabulous.

Her mind wandered back again to two years ago. Once the children were settled into a routine, and Seth managed to work through the initial hurt and disappointment of Felicity leaving, their Mum fell ill. It was cancer and there was no treatment available. Jessica decided to take leave without pay to nurse her Mum and take care of their Dad. The trauma of the family breakdown and his wife being unwell had aged their father. Bill's stature was slumped, his hair thinned and he lost weight. Brother and sister were concerned for his welfare.

The children were the bright spot in their lives, at least, Alicia was. Ryan often withdrew and communicated little. Although, when he was with his Grandad, they cheered each other up. Bill would teach Ryan the basics of growing food. The farmer might have retired but he wanted to share his skills with his grandson. The pair in check shirts, Levi's and Blundstone boots would wander around in the vegetable garden together, and pick the ripened fruit of their labours.

Six months later, Granny, as they called her, was admitted to the hospital for palliative care. Seth and Jessica took turns to sit with their father until the end of Granny's life. The day came when they all said goodbye and she went to be with the Lord.

Tears flowed at the funeral. Family and friends came in droves to farewell the stoic woman. She'd contributed to their community in many ways throughout her lifetime. The Country Women's Association sent the family a magnificent bouquet of banksia, protea and kangaroo paws arranged with Geraldton wax. It arrived with enough food to last at least a week. Neighbours sent cards, flowers and offered condolences in their loss.

It was difficult to believe that two months later, Grandad had a stroke and was paralysed down his left side, he was left-handed and couldn't manage on his own. Jessica had already returned to Perth but came back to care for him. He didn't last long, a massive stroke took him and everyone was in shock. Most thought the loss of his beloved wife had caused him unbearable anxiety and he'd lost the will to live. Another funeral had to be arranged. Everyone pitched in to help them through the difficult days of grieving.

More than a year had gone by since then and life was getting back to normal for Jess. Now, this … what would happen next? She didn't dare ponder that thought for too long.

CHAPTER 10

F lames danced beneath the fondue pots on their tripod stands. Rich, creamy cheeses flavoured with garlic and white wine warmed in a red enamel pot, and smooth, silky dark chocolate simmered in another. Long-handled forks with identifying coloured tips were laid out ready to use. Chunks of crusty bread, cherry tomatoes, diced apple and pear were prepared for the guests. Casseroles of curry, rice, beef stroganoff and apricot chicken completed the banquet. Punch bowls of spicy iced drinks were decorated with orange slices. Dainty glass cups hung off hooks around the perimeter.

Courtney's dream of a smorgasbord style meal had become a reality. Two weeks ago Liam had hauled out boxes of fancy-wrapped wedding gifts. An array of dessert bowls, mixing bowls, sheets, towels and pillowslips with His and Hers embroidered on them had been strewn around the room with casserole dishes and utensils. The fondue pots were Courtney's prize possessions, and she'd been experimenting with recipes to get the right combination in time for her birthday dinner.

Serviettes folded to look like Sydney's Opera House decorated the plates. Three candles on a tall stand in the centre of the table flickered with yellow plumes and illuminated two small vases of flowers. Liam beamed at his 21-year-old wife. Her birthday had been on Thursday, but the gathering was planned for today, Saturday.

"It looks stunning, Courtney." Pride evident in his voice. He wished his parents had been able to come and see this.

"I hope everyone likes it."

Liam broke into song and belted out the jingle from the Meadow Lea television commercial.

'You oughta to be congratulated! Wait until they taste it. You oughta, you oughta be … congratulated."

He squeezed her tight and placed a light kiss on her cheek.

"I know, don't mess with the make-up," he intentionally withdrew from her with his hands up in surrender.

Jacob Hoyle came in through the kitchen door.

"What a wonder you are, Courtney. I'm glad I'm here, it's worth coming all this way just for this magnificent feast," he teased.

He'd been thrilled with the 21st birthday invitation and arrived in Perth from Sydney the day before. He had a speech and presentation to make and appreciated the opportunity for witnesses – or an audience, perhaps. *I'm becoming theatrical,* he thought. So unlike his solicitous, ordered self.

The doorbell rang. Courtney smiled and went to welcome her guests, who lavished her with gifts, hugs, kisses and good wishes. Millie, Todd, Keith, Tom and Annie and the O'Reilly children came on time. Bob and Beryl were close behind them. Twenty minutes later, the doorbell rang again.

"Seth," Courtney acknowledged him, surprised he had a young woman alongside holding Ryan's hand. "Come in."

Alicia, with a huge smile on her face, handed the wrapped box with a large bow to their hostess.

"Happy Birthday, Courtney."

The little girl jumped up and down.

"Open it, come on, open it!"

Her excitement interrupted the introductions that should have been made.

"Okay, come on into the lounge room."

Gifts adorned the table. Courtney carefully undid the ribbon and pulled the sticky tape away, trying not to tear the paper. Alicia rolled her eyes. She would have ripped the paper off if it was her present. Maybe big people, at twenty-one, didn't do that sort of thing. She waited impatiently for the gift to be exposed.

"What's this?" Courtney queried.

Alicia and Ryan both chirped in together.

"Mallee's having puppies … and one of them will be for you."

That explained the dog bowl, a bag of dog biscuits and a red leather collar and lead.

"Well, that's wonderful. I'll get a dog at last."

Excitement pulsed through Courtney, she was thrilled at the prospect.

"See Dad, we knew." Alicia turned back again. "We knew you'd like it but Dad wasn't sure."

"They were right. I'm glad we haven't put you on the spot. I thought it might be more like a white elephant than a red cloud Kelpie. Courtney, my apologies, this is my sister, Jessica. Jess turned up unexpectedly late this afternoon. Liam said she should come, too, when I rang earlier."

Courtney harrumphed.

"He didn't tell me. We were busy and Jacob was already here. It's nice to meet you, Jessica. I'm glad you're here."

"Thanks, and Happy Birthday."

Jessica thought Courtney was lovely. Seth was concerned he might have put his foot in it – maybe he'd better warn Liam that he'd forgotten to tell her Jess was coming. He needn't have worried. Courtney radiated happiness and there was more than enough food.

Todd approached Seth's sister.

"Hello," he said. "Do you remember me?"

Jess took a moment to absorb the face before her.

"Todd York?" her chin dropped and she tilted her head. "Was it Ocean Beach Mission at Denmark? Years ago?"

His face lit up.

"Yes. You were the leader who took us grommets surfing."

"I do remember. You look a bit different now that you've lost the surfie look."

Jessica had loved her role at the several Beach Missions she'd been involved in after Christmas during the school holidays. It had been a long time since then.

"Did you hear that the team had to evacuate from the beach into town this year because of the bushfires?"

"No. That must've been a bit scary."

"I believe the kids thought it was all very exciting."

"That'd be right."

They chatted for a few more minutes before Liam called the gathering to order.

"Thank you for all coming tonight to help celebrate Courtney's 21st Birthday."

He glowed with satisfaction.

"Reverend Bob is going to say grace and then we can enjoy the spread before us."

The kids had already been allowed to have a few things to nibble on. They loved stabbing the bits of bread and dipping it into the hot cheese.

"Okay, folks, let's bow our heads. Heavenly Father, thank you that we have been privileged to be a part of Courtney's life. We give you praise that you have blessed her and Liam. May you continue to guide her in your ways and reveal your will all her days. We thank you for the bountiful food we are about to share and pray you will bless our time together. In Jesus name, Amen."

Courtney looked around her kitchen and dining space. The crowded room was filled with people she loved balancing plates on their knees. Keith sat with Todd and Jessica, all three deep in conversation. Tom and Liam swapped stories, and Annie was chatting to Bob and Beryl. The children sat on the floor at the feet of their parents. There was no better gift than their friendship, and the help they'd given her. She often felt unworthy but Millie assured her that she was a blessing to them too. Her eyes wandered to the little pink china piggy bank sitting in its spot on the mantle above the stove.

Thank you, Uncle Geoff. I had no idea that life could be like this. She felt special, at last, after growing up without any family. *It's all because of you and the Lord's blessing.*

Her attention was drawn back into the circle to pass someone the bread. She could not wipe the smile off her face and didn't want to, either.

Todd looked across the room. Millie and Alicia were examining the contents of the party bag Courtney had given the children. They discovered a lollypop, sherbert packet, a little box of colour pencils, and best of all, a blue and red bug clicker. They experimented with the sounds they could make with it. Their heads were bent close together and Todd noticed the similar profiles, same ponytail at the nape of their neck and heard them chatting happily away. He rolled his lips under and blinked fast a few times to suppress the tears stinging at the back of his eyes. He could see Millie struggled. These events were hard on her, but they agreed that revealing her relationship with Seth had to be in God's timing.

Jacob Hoyle tapped a glass with a spoon to get everyone's attention.

"Ladies and Gentlemen, I'd like to take this opportunity to make a speech concerning our friend, Courtney, on the auspicious occasion of her 21st Birthday."

All eyes turned to the solicitor and they waited quietly.

"Fifteen years ago, I was contacted by Geoffrey Lancaster from Perth in Western Australia. I thought it a little odd he wanted a lawyer in Sydney, New South Wales. After I understood his plight I was compelled to undertake the search to find his nephew's young daughter who, seemingly, had disappeared and could not be found. There were times when I encouraged Geoffrey to give up, but he would not. We tried every avenue we could think of to pursue and continued to follow those leads over and over again."

Jacob paused and sipped water from the glass in front of him. One could imagine him in court proceedings doing just such a thing. The audience refocussed their attention.

"I was devastated when the elderly man became quite ill in his later years. I felt I'd let him down. We had an arrangement whereby I would send a report at the end of each month to state the search processes we'd attempted. He never wavered in his faith that, one day, we would find her."

Courtney choked up with emotion. She had no idea this was going on while her life whiled away in a Children's Home.

"Geoffrey insisted the search continue, using his estate, and all of it if it came down to that, to cover the costs. I could not, in all earnestness, do that. He was right, however, we did find her and here she is settled in Geoffrey's home. I was made Trustee over Courtney's estate, and it now gives me great pleasure to make a special announcement."

The smartly dressed moustached man picked up a metal lockbox and concertina file.

"Courtney, your parents' wills bequeathed their home, property and bank balances for you to receive after you turned twenty-one. I've managed this portfolio on your behalf and today, I hand over the contents of these documents and ownership into your care. I take great joy in wishing you a very Happy Birthday."

Everyone cheered and applauded Jacob for his speech. They enjoyed watching the initial look of confusion, followed by elation emanating from Courtney's face. She received the ominous items with trepidation. Jacob assured her quietly that they would have a discussion to quell her fears. She stood and cleared her throat.

"Thank you, Jacob. I'm stunned and that's happened a lot lately. I want to thank everyone for coming to share my celebration. It has been a privilege to know all of you and become your friend. Yes, including you, Todd."

A titter around the room followed as they all turned and looked at him.

"My life has changed and you have all contributed in many ways. To think, I couldn't even cook a meal before I came here, and now it's one of my favourite pastimes. Thanks especially to you, Millie. You've taught me much more than reading a recipe and I don't know what I would have done without you."

A sheen glistened in her neighbour's eyes.

Answered prayers, many of them, Millie thought.

"And as for Liam, well, all I can say is – I thank God every day for you. And, soon, I will get the puppy I've longed for all my life."

Her eyes sparkled when she looked directly at Alicia and Ryan. Jimmy, Jon and Bronte clapped their hands, sharing in the fun. Courtney placed a white wooden key with a golden number 21 on the table. A fancy biro sat beside it.

"Please remember to sign my key before you leave. You too, kids."

Applause broke out and Annie produced a birthday cake with 21 candles alight ready to be blown out.

"Happy Birthday to you ..." they all sang and bellowed out three cheers.

CHAPTER 11

J acob joined Liam and Courtney for breakfast. He was dressed in casual slacks, a polo shirt and wore moccasins on his feet. He looked relaxed and happy.

"I enjoyed myself last night, Courtney. It was a wonderful evening and I'm so pleased I came. Don't worry about any of those business details. We'll go through it later on and I'll explain it all to you."

"Thanks, Jacob. It's a bit overwhelming. I had no idea my parents had left me a legacy."

She poured him a cup of tea and passed it over.

"You had enough to cope with learning of Geoffrey's estate." He picked up the cup. "I didn't want to alarm you with knowledge of the other at the time."

"Thanks. That was a good decision and I'm grateful. It's hard enough to take in now."

"May I come along to church with you this morning?"

The solicitor had found the good people from this community to be stable friends for his client, and he marvelled at the way they communicated with each other. Liam and Courtney were pleased with his request. Jacob had planned to stay with them for several days and didn't have to rush off.

"Of course."

He went to dress for church, in his usual suit, tie, pocket-handkerchief and wearing shiny shoes.

Millie had been up early beseeching her Heavenly Father and pouring out the anguish that lay deep within her heart.

"Oh, Father, I can't bear having to keep silent. Seth is my son, Lord, our son, Harold's and mine. I only want to be a part of his life. It's not fair, well, it's not that it isn't fair really, it's just heartbreaking that he doesn't know. Will he ever get to know, Lord? Can he ever be told the truth?"

Memories of the evening before, the church services and meals Seth had attended over the past months flashed before her.

"And my precious grandchildren, to think that I have grandchildren, you have blessed me to meet them. I'm not complaining, Lord, Your grace will be sufficient for me. I know that, but I'm weak and I can't put on a brave face without your help. Even though it's wonderful, it's exhausting. I can't believe you allowed our paths to cross after such a long time. Oh, the tearing apart I experienced when I had to let him go. Time never took the ache away. My arms were emptied and never filled, but he had people who loved him and nurtured him. I give you praise, dear Lord, praise for your goodness to us. Praise for your unfailing love and forgiveness. Take my weakness and replace it with your strength. I pray in Jesus name, Amen."

Millie struggled up from her kneeling position on the mat beside her bed and stood. She wiped away the dampness at her eyes with a tissue tucked in her sleeve. Millie dressed, picked up her Bible and headed out the door to go to church.

Reverend Bob made the regular announcements to the congregation, and included congratulations to Courtney for her significant birthday. His message was from Isaiah 40:31. The words were a balm to Millie; 'but those who hope in the Lord will renew their strength. They will soar on wings like eagles; they will run and not grow weary, they will walk and not be faint.'

"Life gets hard sometimes," Bob said. "Waiting on the Lord can be difficult but it is never a waste of time. He might be preparing us, or someone close to us, for purposes we don't understand. God intends to renew your strength, to lift you and recharge your batteries. It may be in some seemingly insignificant way or, it may be a massive blessing he bestows upon you. Whatever it is, ask God for his help and trust him to deliver. The day will come when you can soar in your situation. When you walk in a valley, or rise to the crest of the hill with the ups and downs of life - trust him to be your strength. You will manage to get past the walking stage, to run and fly and soar on wings like eagles. 'Trust and Wait' is the message I want you to take home with you today."

Bob finished the service with a prayer and a hymn. Millie grasped God's word to her hurting heart. She knew it, she'd heard it all before, but today it had a special meaning.

"Hi Millie," Todd approached her. "Today's message sounds a bit familiar."

His broad smile lifted her spirits.

"You're right, Todd. Trust and wait, that's what I need to do."

She was encouraged remembering Todd's recent experience of having to wait on the Lord. It was she, remarkably, who had prompted him to do just that. Now it was her turn and she felt renewed strength fill her being.

"You decided to come here today instead of going into Albany."

Todd wasn't sure if that was a question or a statement.

"After a late night, I thought a bit longer in bed would be nice for a change."

He waved at Courtney and Liam, excused himself and went to speak to them. Millie was surprised he'd had a late night. They'd all left about ten o'clock. *Hmmm, I wonder* ... then she pulled herself up. *That will not do, Millie, stop surmising and let it be,* she reprimanded herself.

The lockbox held a set of keys, a title deed and two bank books. The folder had documents outlining shares for Pilbardi Iron Ore Mining Company and several other companies of various interests.

"We're rich, Liam, look at this."

Courtney passed the bank books over to her husband.

"Phew," he gasped. "I'm glad I married you."

They laughed and shook their heads in disbelief.

"A four-bedroom, two-bathroom brick and tile house in Applecross, with views of the Swan River. Sounds posh." Liam enthused. "If your parents had lived, you might have had hordes of brothers and sisters to fill that house." He paused. "Such a shame."

Courtney lifted the folder and perused the photographs of the different rooms and the front view of the place her parent's had called home. Jacob had a Perth street directory with the page earmarked to show them where it was. It was rented to a couple four years ago. A real estate company managed the rental agreement and it was still valid. They were good tenants and happy for a long-term lease.

"Jacob, I don't think I understand what's involved with the shares. Would you be willing to continue to manage it for us? We could take the house and property on board, if you think so, Liam?" she asked.

Liam nodded in agreement.

"Absolutely." Jacob shared a personal story. "I had a dream when I was a boy that I would grow up to work on the Australian Stock Exchange floor. That was until I realised how noisy, chaotic and dangerous it was."

"Dangerous?" Liam queried.

"Oh, I meant for the chalkies who walk on that precarious ledge; the ones who erase and alter figures on the board. I'm sure someone must have tumbled off there every so often. But, no, it wasn't for me. Far too disorderly for my liking. That's why I became a lawyer, it being a much more controlled environment. It suits me better."

Jacob was happy to maintain his association with Courtney and Liam, which he thought was more about their developing friendship than the money he'd earn. He had an emotional investment and he wasn't prepared to let it go. Geoffrey's faithful witness to him over the years had continued to nag at him that God did exist and He cared for him.

"I enjoyed the service today. Thank you for letting me come along."

"It was our pleasure."

"There is a church near where I live in Mosman. I've heard pipe organ music playing when I've gone for a walk past it. I might go in there when I go home, and check it out, as you would say."

He smiled.

I don't think these modern sayings suit me, either, he thought, *try as I might, to fit in.*

CHAPTER 12

Todd roared down Millie's driveway and slammed on the brakes. It frightened her when she heard the unexpected loud noise out the back.

"Millie," he called through the flywire screen door, "can I come in?"

It was a workday. He wore his new khaki shorts and shirt with 'Yorkie's Home Help' commercially embroidered above the pocket. When she came to the door he removed his boots and apologised about his smelly socks.

"What's all this about?"

Millie came straight to the point.

"I had to come and tell you. I just had to."

His blue eyes danced with excitement.

"I had a dream, no, more a vision."

"Really?" she questioned the validity of what he was saying.

"Yes. And, I believe it was from the Lord, and ..." he took another breath "... you are gonna love it."

"Really?" Millie reiterated, shifting her attitude.

Oh, to be so enthusiastic about life. She'd nearly forgotten how that felt. *Never mind.*

"So tell me," and she went to put the kettle on.

Always, and ever, Millie would make a cup of tea. It was one of life's ever-present staples in her opinion. And a biscuit to go with it, of course.

"Okay, you know how I told you I had a late-night on Saturday? And that was why I came to church at All Saints on Sunday?"

"Ye-es," she hesitated, remembering her thoughts about that.

"Well, after I got home on Saturday, I felt the Spirit of the Lord prompt me to pray for you. You'll be proud of me, Millie. I was obedient and spent hours praying for you, and Seth and the kids. Intercessory prayer."

"Wow, you did that for me?"

"Yep, and I know the Spirit is moving, Millie. God's going to sort out your situation for you. I feel a bit like Daniel, you know, getting dreams and interpreting them. Except I'm not sure about some of the interpretation of my dream."

"Go on," the older woman encouraged him not to get side-tracked.

"Some of it might sound a bit odd but I'll tell you anyway."

"Please do."

Anticipation was making her edgy. What was Todd going to come out with?

"So, there you are standing in a field with a baby in your arms ..." he paused. "And a strong wind came along and whipped the babe away. Then you were in a valley, and it was dark and foreboding, but someone reached out and led you up a rough path. It was Harold, Millie. I saw him."

Tears silently slipped down her life-worn skin.

"But there's more … you both stood on a mountaintop and it was like you were glued together, strengthening each other. You were smiling, Millie. Then a cloud came down and covered the mountain. You were both hidden and when the fog lifted, you were by yourself, alone but not unhappy."

"Oh, Todd, that's my life in a nutshell. How interesting."

He put his arm across and touched her hand.

"Don't say anything more just yet; hear me out first."

A weak smile formed on her lips.

"A farmhouse appeared in a paddock, a bit like the field you were in before. Except now a family was outside. Then a wind came along, it whipped around the house and tore the family apart. Darkness surrounded the house, but a shaft of light pierced the sky and shone directly into it."

Seth. That would be Seth. Alone with the children but learning to trust in God.

Millie shifted in her seat and wiped the perspiration from her hands on a tissue.

"It's harder to work this bit out. Thunder and lightning filled the sky. People stood around a fire, trying to get warm and dry. I couldn't see who they were but you were at home on your knees, praying."

What could it mean?

"I woke up, in the dream, I mean, and after the storm I found you and took your hand and placed it in Seth's. Your son smiled, and, he glowed. Like an aura around him, I think."

Does that mean he dies and I get to see him in heaven? He doesn't find out I'm his mother until we get to glory? Oh, but that's not the way I want it to be.

"The children are walking along, holding your hand and looking up at you with smiles on their faces. And then I did wake up. It seemed real, Millie. I'm sure there is a message in it for you. What do you think?"

Todd's look was intense. She didn't want to share those last thoughts with him. It would be far too distressing.

"I'm dumbfounded, Todd. It would seem you have, indeed, had a vision. I wouldn't like to guess what it all means but I agree that God has to have a hand in it. One might even go so far as to say that more may be revealed in time, either soon or maybe later on."

Todd's head nodded enthusiastically.

"I felt sure you would want to know, Millie."

She smiled at the young man, even though it had been a bit disturbing, it was kind of him to share it with her.

"I have a confession to make," Todd added.

"A confession?"

What now?

"I used to call you 'the old biddy.' It was a rude and immature thing to do."

Millie laughed out loud.

"You didn't?"

"Yep, I did, and I'm sorry. You are an amazing woman and I know my Mum has always appreciated your friendship. She rebuked me for saying such a thing, but I only ever did it at home or in my head."

Millie laughed again.

"You were a child, Todd. Children do that sort of thing."

"Things changed that day, though, when I heard your story. I had compassion for you. At least as much compassion as a teenage boy can muster."

Well, I never.

"I'm interested to know, Todd, what you did hear?"

He looked up and thought for a minute.

"It's vague. I remember the bit about you being young and that it only happened once, and you fell pregnant. That explains what you said to me about a one-night-stand."

Millie became defensive, her shame lifting after hearing talk about her situation at the time.

"It wasn't a one-night-stand, Todd."

"Oh, how come you told Mum that, then?"

He was confused.

"We waited and got married. There was never anyone else."

"So you mean it only happened once before you married each other."

"Yes, that's what I mean. I didn't go around having sex with men as a favourite pastime."

Todd was about to take offence. It wasn't what he had inferred.

"Sorry. I'm being silly. It was a long time ago, but Harold and me, we only ever loved one another. There were no other romances. We were pushed apart by our parents after they discovered I was pregnant and forbade us to see each other. It was legal to marry at 21 without parental permission. We planned to elope on my birthday but it was a long wait. That's the valley you saw in the vision, I think."

His compassion returned.

"We couldn't have any more children."

Her voice was soft and devastatingly sad.

"We tried but had seven miscarriages. That brought us closer together, but for some people it tears them apart. Every year we grew closer and closer. I loved that man so much and I thank God for the blessing of the time we had together. I miss him, but my cherished memories are never far away."

"Wow, I had no idea you went through all that pain. God's light shines from you, Millie. You're a great encouragement to me and a lot of other people."

"Thanks, Todd. I learned from my mistake and I understand how easy it is to fall into sin. At the time, I felt I'd let my Lord down but his grace goes beyond all bounds. I've only ever wanted to be in His will."

Her fingers drummed on the tablecloth, making a soft padded thudding sound. He could see her mind's eye whirring. He waited.

"Do you think Seth ... I don't know, will he ... when he finds out, do you think he'll forgive me?"

CHAPTER 13

July 29 loomed large before Seth. He did not want to go to Perth and did not want to attend the court case. His lawyer suggested that it would be in his best interest to go. Jessica agreed to come to the farm and take care of the family and animals while he was away. They would do a house swap and he'd stay in her flat in Perth.

The drive to the city felt interminable. Dread washed over him. His stomach was in knots and his head ached with the stress of the whole situation. He wanted it to be over and done with so he could get back to his routine, uninteresting life.

He fought with the yellow and blue striped tie after the frustration of buttoning down the collar on his dark blue shirt. The lawyer had told him to wear smart clothes to the courtroom. *Did he think I'd turn up in farm jeans and a fleecy check shirt? I'm not that stupid.* The tie was yanked off. He started again and knotted it with success the next time.

Stay calm. Breathe deep and don't get angry. Instructions whirled around in Seth's head. Pay attention. You probably won't need to say anything, but if the judge asks you a question, give him a clear answer. Take your time, don't blurt out anything that might hinder the judge's assessment of you. *I should have asked Liam or Keith to come with me but I couldn't do it. I'm humiliated enough as it is.*

"Remember to stand when the judge comes in," his lawyer whispered.

The final hearing was held in the Probate and Family Court even though it was an uncontested case. The proceedings began. Confirmation of the divorce application filed on no-fault grounds simplified the process. Both parties acknowledged being Australian citizens living permanently within the country, and the same state of Western Australia.

Seeing Felicity dressed in a navy skirt and white shirt with a navy blazer looking demure but with a fierce glint in her eyes almost undid Seth. The man, Oliver, he presumed, sat in a dark grey suit behind her. He leaned over several times and tapped Felicity on the shoulder to discuss a point with her. She responded with a nod each time.

The judge addressed Felicity. It was an informal hearing and the judge's prerogative to elect which approach he would take.

"Ms Norman, may I call you Felicity?"

"Yes, sir."

She stood at her lawyer's suggestion.

"Are you certain that there is no possibility of restoring your marriage to Seth Jarvis?"

"None, your Honour."

"I see you have been separated for more than the one-year requirement."

He shuffled papers in front of him.

"Tell me what you have been doing in the last couple of years."

"Sir, I actively set out to achieve my goal of a prestigious career in Education. This year I was appointed Deputy Principal at Perth Girls' College."

"So, you would say you're successful and content in your work?"

"Yes, sir, I love my job."

"Thank you. You may be seated."

The judge turned his attention to Seth.

"Seth, you would prefer a reconciliation, is that correct?"

He stood.

"Yes, sir."

Seth's gut churned with nervousness.

"You're a farmer in the south-west. Sheep, and grain." He looked up over the top of his glasses at Seth. "Have you been farming long?"

"Yes, sir." Seth paused; he wasn't sure what he should say. "We have a property that's been in the family for three generations."

The judge nodded and shuffled through some more paperwork.

"You have agreed to the divorce with the understanding that this is what Felicity desires."

"Yes, sir."

Seth felt light-headed. *Breathe*, he prompted himself.

"Very well, please, sit down."

Perhaps the judge noticed his pallor and was concerned he might fall if he didn't sit soon.

Seven years, that's all they'd been married for, not long in the scheme of things. Seth sighed. How would the judge settle their property issues. Surely he couldn't lose the farm. The thought hadn't occurred to him that it was a possibility. What if Felicity wanted half of it? He didn't have enough capital to pay her off. Things were getting worse, but Seth didn't think she would expect that, in fairness to him. He didn't know her anymore. Being here proved the point.

The judge spoke again.

"I deem the farming property is to be ..." he was distracted by Oliver speaking over him to Felicity. Seth caught the words 'you've got a right to have a share of it' and 'don't let it go.' Felicity's lawyer interrupted them, annoyed with their conversation. The judge coughed and Oliver and Felicity turned their attention back to the front of the courtroom. He glared at them. Felicity reddened.

"I repeat, I deem the farming property to remain solely in Seth Tawnya Jarvis' possession. It is vital that our farmers are supported in their commitment to providing food for our nation. I thank you, Seth, and your past family members for working the land to our advantage."

He spoke with authority. Oliver scowled and tapped Felicity on the shoulder. The judge looked at him with a dark stare to dare him to interfere again. Oliver slid back on his seat and folded his arms. Relief flooded through Seth.

"Given that you were married for seven years, I do, however, think that the work carried out by Felicity in the family home should be recognised. Seth, the court orders payment of $5,000 to be made as recompense."

Oliver was shocked, his loud 'Huh' echoed in the quiet room. The man sat shaking his head. He went to lean forward again.

"I don't know who you are, sir, but I am going to ask you to leave the courtroom. Your disruptions could lead me to charging you with contempt of court."

Felicity was embarrassed.

"Just go," she whispered.

Her frustration was evident as he rose, he was making things worse. Admittedly, it seemed a paltry sum in her eyes, but it was better than nothing. If Oliver stayed in the room, she might not get anything at all.

"Now, regarding the matter of the children," the judge looked to Seth's lawyer, "do you need a moment with your client?"

"Yes, your Honour, I do."

"Very well, we will take a short recess and resume proceedings in, say, fifteen minutes."

"Thank you, sir, that will be long enough."

Seth was shell-shocked. The kids, no, she can't have the kids. Where did this come from? There was no mention of it before the case commenced. They walked out of the courtroom. Felicity and Oliver were having a heated discussion by a water fountain.

"Seth, come on. We have a meeting room available through here."

The lawyer shadowed his client into the room. A bright fluorescent tube in the ceiling illuminated the dark cream walls and reflected light off the glossy wood grain Laminex desk.

"What is this all about? I didn't know ..." his voice rose, anger creeping in.

His hand gripped the back of the chair, his knees weak.

"Hang on, Seth." His lawyer interrupted him. "Felicity Norman's solicitor threw this on me this morning as we walked into the hearing. It's not according to the protocol of the law; we can delay dealing with it today. Another hearing before the Family Court will need to be made." He puffed out a breath of exasperation. "It's unethical to do this to any lawyer and emotionally cruel to you."

"I can't lose my kids. I just can't."

"I know it's hard to accept but I don't want you to worry about it now. We can work out the details later."

Seth broke down. He'd only just managed to hold himself together, but this was too heavy a burden to bear.

CHAPTER 14

The Royal Wedding beamed across the world to 750 million viewers. Seth Jarvis did not count among that number. Jessica's flat was warm and homely and a good investment for the Hakea Hollow Farm Trust. It could have been lost today but the judge made the right call. *Felicity must be earning a packet in her new job. The illustrious Oliver unwittingly did us all a favour, if he'd kept his mouth shut I might be feeling worse than I do. I'd almost lay a bet on him being the one to bring the kids into the fray.* His mind was worn out and his heart was sore. He'd bought some take-away food, but couldn't face it. It ended up in the bin, untouched.

Popcorn hit the frypan lid with loud pitting noises, and the kids were ecstatic. Jessica decided to let Ryan and Alicia stay up and witness the wedding of Prince Charles to Lady Diana Spencer. It was a significant moment in the British royal family history and they should remember it at their ages. Jess found it was a good distraction from worrying about her brother's court case.

Todd had rung the night before for a chat. He planned to come and have dinner with Jess and the children. Spaghetti Bolognese sauce simmered on the stove. A pot of boiling water had the pasta added to it. Grated cheese was piled up ready to put on top when it was done.

"It smells yummy in here."

Todd sniffed the air when he walked through the door.

"The telly's on, and we've got popcorn and lime cordial," Alicia announced.

Jessica stirred the pot.

"She's been humming 'here comes the bride' all afternoon. Ryan just about went nuts listening to it until I sang, 'Here comes the bride all dressed in white, she slipped on a banana peel and went for a ride.' The kids were in fits of laughter and they made a skit out of it. Alicia is an actress in the making, Todd. I'm sure she'd oblige you with another performance."

Dinner was dished up and they got comfortable on the couch to watch the drama in London unfold. The streets from Clarence House to St Paul's Cathedral were crowded with spectators. The buzz among the people was almost tangible. Carriage after carriage, drawn by regally adorned horses, rode past. Royalty waved and people applauded as the spectacle went by. Prince Charles arrived in a gold-encrusted coach, and a roar went up as he stepped down to enter the cathedral.

"Here she comes."

The glass coach with Lady Diana and her father, Lord John Spencer approached the church.

Alicia jumped up and down on the spot several times.

"Oooh, it's like a fairy tale. Look at the dress, it's so big and puffy."

Ryan poked his sister.

"She's a real princess, Leesh, not a pretend one like in your books."

"Come on, Alicia, sit down and eat your dinner. The bride is going to walk up the aisle now with her father. We better watch just in case she slips … on a banana peel."

The kids joined in with the last few words, giggling and singing the ditty again. Lady Diana took three and a half minutes to walk the length of the aisle at St Paul's before the ceremony began.

An hour later, both children were fast asleep. Todd picked up Ryan and Jess collected Alicia to carry them to their beds. Their aunt tucked them in and turned off the lights.

"I'm exhausted," Jess admitted to Todd. "I had no idea that two days of kids would wear me out so easily."

"Yeah, well, you're not getting any younger, you know."

Todd grinned at the 'older woman' sitting beside him.

"Like you're so young yourself. How old are you now?"

"Still under thirty," Todd stated with a twinkle in his eye.

"Oh, yes, you're such a baby. I have to say, though, my extra years do make a difference."

"On a more serious note, have you heard from Seth today?"

Jessica shook her head.

"No, I suspect it was probably too hard for him to talk about it yet."

There was a quiet lull in the conversation.

"Yeah, us blokes don't communicate our feelings that well. Not like women do, they seem to be able to blurt it out to their friends and no-one minds."

Jess snorted and sent a look of disgust his way.

"What a terrible thing to say. Even if it is true."

Seth arrived at the farm, jumped out of the car and stretched. It was good to be home after the effort it had taken to get through the day before. He'd had a restless night with only an hour or so of deep sleep. The events in the courtroom kept going through his mind, reliving the whole scene over and over. Not that he wanted to, but it wouldn't go away.

"I'm glad you're home," Jess went out to meet him. She'd heard the car drive up and was relieved to know he was safe.

"Hi Tati, thanks for taking care of the kids for me."

"You know I don't mind. I wish it were for a different reason. How did it go?"

Seth shared the details with her and they commiserated at the sad demise of his marriage. The pair were thankful that their property was spared and shed tears at the prospect of facing Family Court again to settle an arrangement about Ryan and Alicia.

"I'm afraid, Jess. Mothers usually get the children in these situations."

"Yeah, but don't forget Felicity left with a screed about why she was leaving and how you were the best person to parent her children."

He'd forgotten about the letter. He would have to try and find it to see if the lawyer could use it as evidence in court.

"And you have God on your side."

It doesn't feel much like it, but I know she's right.

Ryan and Alicia were all over their Dad when they got home from school. They'd missed him even if it was only for two days. He revelled in the attention they showered on him.

Seth walked into the closed room that had been his father's study. It was neat and tidy, unlike his own. They'd shared the house before Felicity had come along. Once they were married, his parent's bought a house in town but kept the office at the farm.

"I know Dad hid that letter in here somewhere so the kids would never find it. Where would he have put it?"

He spoke into the empty void hoping to conjure up an answer to his question. Seth sat at his Dad's desk and memories assailed him. So much had happened in the last few years that it was just as well he didn't know what the future held back then. He was drained in every way. Emotionally, physically and spiritually – just getting through one day was hard work.

The desk, it was in the desk somewhere, the thought occurred to him. Seth pulled out drawers and lifted neat stacks of paperwork to check underneath. *I need to sort this out, there's stuff in here we don't need for tax purposes anymore. Don't get distracted; find that letter.*

"I know. Dad had a secret compartment put into the desk to secure important documents."

He spoke quietly to himself, tapping his feet on the floor. *Where was it? Remember. Come on, think, Seth.*

His mind worked overtime while he felt around for false bottoms on drawers, knocking to hear for a hollow space. He pulled the desk away from the wall.

"Aha." Bingo, a hinged sheet of ply with a panel clip holding it in place lay over a portion at the back. Seth pulled the clip aside and the sheeting was released. Several documents were exposed and the envelope with Felicity's handwriting was at the front.

"Gotcha," he commented. Relief at finding it washed over him.

The title deed for the farm was in there with his parents' passports, marriage certificate and a full birth certificate for Jessica. *Where's mine?* An envelope with the farm's address sat behind all the other documents. Seth pulled it out, opened it and paled at the sight of a Consent to the Adoption of a Child papers.

Adoption Form 3.

Family Court of Western Australia

I, Millicent Elizabeth Glendalow of 10 Lord Street, East Perth

Minor, hereby consent to making of an order of adoption in respect of

Male Child

The form went on to explain that agreeing to the adoption of the child, she would permanently be deprived of her rights as a mother.

His date of birth written beside 'this child' of no name, born in Perth, shocked him to the core. A notice of revocation was stated as being understood by the mother with a 30-day opportunity to revoke the adoption order. The father of the child was marked as unknown.

Her signature at the bottom of the page witnessed by a Justice of the Peace left him reeling. A birth certificate for adopted children was attached to the form with his name and bearing his adoptive parents' names – William Albert and Anastasia Jarvis.

He'd thought they were his Mum and Dad, but they weren't. Not his biological parents. A surge of resentment and anger toward them came from deep within. *How dare they? Why did they never tell me?* He had to get out of here. The documents were dropped on the floor and Seth took flight.

"Tawny, did you find the letter?" Jessica asked.

"I don't know why Mum and Dad gave me the name Tawnya when I don't have any Russian in me, and they aren't my parents anyway. You're not even my sister."

Jessica was confused. What was he going on about?

The door pushed against the dog as he stormed through it.

"Get out of the way, Mallee."

Jessica witnessed the angry display and was distressed by her brother's behaviour.

"Seth! Be careful, she's pregnant. Don't be so mean."

He flashed a look behind as he walked away with an element of remorse at being so cruel. Life was cruel, he'd discovered that in so many ways lately. He didn't care, he didn't know who he was, and nobody wanted him. He strode out into the paddock and kept walking.

Jessica let him go. Her father's study door was open and the light was still on. She saw the documents strewn across the floor and found what had upset him. Tears streamed down her face, poor Tawny. *I don't care, he's still my brother.*

CHAPTER 15

Jessica paced back and forth in the passageway waiting for Seth to return. He'd been gone for over two hours and it was nearly midnight. It would be a waste of time trying to look for him in the dark. She had no idea where he might have gone.

At 1.00am, Jess woke with a start. She'd fallen asleep on the couch in the lounge room, and was aroused when Seth dropped a knife on the tiled floor in the kitchen while making something to eat. Even though the light was on in the other room he hadn't realised Jessica was in there.

He heard her come through the swinging louvre doors.

"Seth, I was worried about you."

She approached him with reticence.

"Sorry."

His eyes were swollen and red, and his voice husky. Jess couldn't decide whether or not to tell him she found the adoption papers. She'd put them back where they were when he left. Her instinct was to say nothing.

"I'm going to bed."

"Okay."

Seth remained at the kitchen sink and didn't turn when she left the room. He would have hugged her, before, when she was his sister. Now he felt alone, bereft. The dishes sat on the sink to drain after he'd rinsed them and he went to his room.

"I want to climb Bluff Knoll[4]."

Seth looked at Jessica with a coolness she'd never experienced from him.

"And camp out for the night."

"Okay, go. I'll stay and look after the children. It's not a problem."

Jess wasn't sure if it was a good idea for him to go alone, but he needed to do this and she couldn't think of a better way to help him. Seth packed his gear and drove off toward the Stirling Range[5] after Alicia and Ryan got on the school bus. He didn't want them to know he was going away again so soon. They'd find out from Jessica when they came home in the afternoon.

The drive along Salt River Road helped to soften his hardened heart. The area was beautiful at this time of the year. The winter rains refreshed the indigenous brush of the Stirling Range National Park and crops on the other side of the road looked green and healthy. The looming mounds of the ranges drew him forward. He pulled into the car park at Bluff Knoll and sat looking at the rise of metamorphic rock before him. It was majestic.

---

4 Bluff Knoll
5 Stirling Range

Words from Psalm 121 found their way through the fog in his mind. 'I lift my eyes up to the mountains. Where does my help come from? My help comes from the Lord, the Maker of heaven and earth'... the roar of a 42-seat coach pulled into the car park and interrupted the moment. Seth groaned.

Maybe if it was a group of older people, he could set off and avoid contact with them, except on the way back down. *I'd rather not pretend to be nice.* A middle-aged woman with a clipboard stepped off the coach and stood at the door. A throng of high school students poured out. *That settles it,* he turned the key on and reversed to leave. He wasn't in the mood for their noise and silly antics when he needed space to contemplate the turmoil he was experiencing. His plan to climb Bluff Knoll and camp at the Stirling Range Caravan Park for the night was thwarted but the idea of camping out on the mountain appealed to him. He'd climb the half ridge walk instead.

Seth parked the car at Gnowellen Road and planned to walk along the firebreak to reach the Ellen's Peak track.

"Okay, I'm not prepared for this," he grimaced as he spoke to himself. "I'll take the bedroll; there goes my comfortable sleep in the swag."

He rustled around, deciding what else he might need.

At least I don't have to worry about disturbing snakes at this time of the year.

"I'll take the rope, and put the small first aid kit in the backpack with the other stuff. That'll do."

The sun was shining but he tied the sleeves of his showerproof jacket around his waist. He'd need it later. The breeze had a bit of a chill and as he climbed it would get colder. It was a clear day with no sign of bad weather, yet he knew that could change suddenly. He and

Reverend Bob had done the Ridge Walk in spring for several years. He smiled. Bob was a lot slower last year but they enjoyed the pace and found more spectacular wildflowers because of it.

He knew being here would ease his pain. Seth strode out at a good pace for the several kilometres to reach the track. His muscles were warm and stretched and ready for the demanding climb ahead. Thoughts shifted back and forth about the discovery of his parentage.

Why didn't they tell me?

Would it be easier for me to understand the truth of it if they had?

Although, I might've grown up being a different kind of person if I'd known.

Ellen's Peak loomed ahead rising 1,012m above the mallee-heath and shale outcrops which he clambered across to begin the steep ascent. There was no clear track in this wilderness zone, although patches of a trail appeared now and then between the uneven surfaces. Piles of rocks built by other climbers were used as markers along the way.

Breathing deeply and actively concentrating on where he placed his feet, Seth felt the benefit of the physical exertion easing his mind. He'd set off much later than anticipated and after three hours his stomach growled with hunger pangs. He hadn't even nibbled at his trail mix of nuts and dried fruit in the side pocket of his backpack. A wide ledge a little further along would be a good place to stop and eat his lunch. It would fuel his body for the next challenging stage of the walk.

The sandwich was a bit squashed after the rope had been shoved in on top of it without giving it a second thought. Jessica had made a massive ham and salad sandwich for him when she'd made the kids' lunches. Come to think of it, she had put the bag of scroggin nibbles together as well, looking out for his welfare. Guilt washed over him. He'd told her she wasn't his sister without any explanation. The thought of her not belonging to him caused a stinging sensation behind his nose and brought tears to his eyes. He didn't want to lose control of his emotions again.

Breathe, look around you.

A still small voice came to mind.

Is that you, Lord?

Seth looked around, almost searching to find a burning bush as Moses had in the Old Testament. What he did see was peace; a contrast to the days of anguish he'd been going through.

Yes, son. I am with you wherever you go.

Help me, Lord, please.

Seth sat contemplating his confused thoughts for twenty minutes before he needed to keep moving along the rough trail. He wanted to make it as far as he could before it got dark and find a camping spot for the night. His compass reading pointed him in the right direction and he headed off.

Leading, guiding. That's what I'll do for you if you let me.

There it was again.

It's not up to me, is it, Lord?

Questioning God wasn't something Seth ever did. Until now.

My grace is sufficient for thee.

Grace? What do I need grace for?

To forgive, as you have been forgiven.

That hit home.

I have to forgive Felicity for leaving me; forgive her and Oliver for wanting to play a part in Alicia and Ryan's lives; forgive Ana and Bill Jarvis for deceiving me, and forgive my birth-mother for giving me away.

The winter solstice had only been ten days ago and the light held on a little longer than it had last week. Seth dug around in his backpack, pulled out his cold dinner and ate greedily. By sunset he rolled out his mat and sat to watch the display in the evening sky. Pale blue turned into a golden glow with deep purple outlining the horizon, then darkness fell.

Seth lay on his bedroll trying to find a comfortable position. Loose shale rocks moved as he wriggled into place. His mind churned with anger at the injustice of his situation but the words 'grace' and 'forgiveness' kept echoing back at him like a clanging gong. He gave up trying to sleep and sat up.

Except for the quiet words earlier in the day, it had been some weeks since Seth had spent any time praying. It had been too hard and confusing. He didn't know what to pray.

'… FOR WE KNOW NOT WHAT WE SHOULD PRAY FOR AS WE OUGHT: BUT THE **SPIRIT** ITSELF MAKETH INTERCESSION FOR US WITH GROANINGS WHICH CANNOT BE UTTERED.' The old King James Version of the Bible memory verse popped into his head.

"So, Lord, maybe the Holy Spirit has been praying for me. Is that why I'm here? To find you in a place that draws me close to you?"

Golden stars dotted the darkened sky. The silence of the night was interrupted by a scuttling noise nearby. Seth smiled, knowing he was among nature where God reigned. It was good for his soul.

"I want to forgive them, Father God, but I don't want to let go of feeling sorry for myself. It's like nobody ever wanted me, it's all broken promises and lies. Don't I have a right to feel rejected and alone?"

I was rejected and alone. They didn't believe me and they took my life. A life I was willing to give up for you and anyone who would trust me for their salvation.

That jolted Seth into remorse, deep remorse.

I have so much to be thankful for and these things do affect other people, not just me.

"I'm sorry, Lord, I can't bear being separated from you. Please forgive me for my wrong attitude and wallowing in self-pity. Take away the hurt and bitterness. I don't want it to be the centre of my life. I forgive Felicity for leaving me and breaking our vow to love each other until one of us would die. As for this Oliver fellow, I still don't like him but I forgive him for being the man Felicity prefers over me."

He laughed out loud.

"Can I say that, Lord? I'm just being honest here."

Bob had told him that God had a sense of humour. After all, we're created in his image and we like to have a laugh.

"Mum and Dad, oh boy, what can I say? They were my parents, they loved me unconditionally, nurtured me all my life and I've repaid their memory with anger. Forgive me for taking my hurt out on Jess. I punished her out of rage at the unfairness of all this because she has their blood in her veins and I don't. Please, Lord, I pray Jess will forgive me."

Tears wet the sides of his face as he spoke freely to the God of the universe, God of his life, God of love and forgiveness.

"Now, the big one … my birth-mother. It shocked me that Felicity could leave her children like she did but my mother, my real mother, let me go as a baby. She never knew me. Did she ever wonder about me? Why did she give me away? Was it her choice? Whatever it was, I forgive her too. I'm trusting you to show me a way forward in my life with its changes and challenges. I give it all to you."

Peace flooded through him. Joy sprung up in his heart and seeped through his being. He lay down and slept soundly.

CHAPTER 16

Seth was chilled to the bone as the sun rose in the eastern sky. His body ached from the effort of the climb the day before. He usually hiked up Bluff Knoll, Mt Trio and Toolbrunup over three weekends to train for the three-day Ridge Walk[6]. No training this time and he was feeling it.

It was a hard slog to reach the summit of Ellen's Peak. When he got there, he took in the scene around him. It was breathtaking. He could see across the top of the rugged range and a patchwork of paddocks in the farmland below. It never ceased to impress him, although he had to admit it was prettier in the wildflower season.

Cloud settled around the stark cliff faces, wisps and swirls decorating Pyungoorup Peak. The descent passing below the southern cliff to Baker's Knob varied from sheltered gullies to climbs and twists and turns in steep loose shale.

It would take a good 12 hours to hike across and use the exit route at First Arrow down to the North Milpunda track. He'd ration his food to last until his descent but his water supply was getting low. It was supposed to have been a one-day climb and night at a campsite, not on the mountain.

---

6 Stirling's Ridge Walk

Seth's efforts waned from time to time. Steep, slippery descents wore on his knees and ankles. Scaling rocky ledges made his hands ache from pulling his weight up when there was little foot leverage. When he could anchor the rope, he'd used it. At midday, he stopped for a snack break and looked back toward the territory he'd covered. He was pleased with his progress. The wind had become stronger and clouds sat low on Ellen's Peak. *That could become a problem,* he thought.

The bag of scroggin provided the energy he needed. Jessica had put carob, almonds, walnuts, sultanas, dried apricots and some boiled lollies in the mix. She'd packed three chocolate bars as well. He put his hand in and took out some more to nibble on and discovered a small folded note. Jessica's handwriting was tiny and neat.

'Seth, I saw your birth certificate. Just so you know, it makes no difference to me. I love you and need you. Always and forever, your sister.' It was signed by Jess, with a love heart.

He puffed out a huge breath and put his head in his hands. Seth had a good cry. Her note released the anxiety of facing her when he got back.

The weather turned nasty. As he passed close by the occasional Stirling Range Banksia[7], the wind whipped the scrubby branches into his face or hands. The sharp edges of the tough serrated leaves bit into his skin. Dark clouds hung low, threatening to drop their load. Seth paused to take another compass reading to continue towards Third Arrow peak. He decided he should step up his pace.

That was a big mistake, on his descent he lost his footing, rolled his ankle and slid several metres down the slope.

---

7 Stirling Range Banksia

"That could have been disastrous," he spoke out loud looking over a ledge where he balanced precariously near a drop that fell a long way below. Seth managed to sidle away from the jagged edge to haul himself up safely.

"Oh, no."

Pain shot through his ankle. *Keep going.* His common sense prevailed in the fog of the increasing discomfort. He struggled to put any weight on that foot and limped along slowly.

"Great. Now I'll be out here another night."

Rain began to fall, and it wasn't long before Seth was soaked to the skin.

Third Arrow had taken hours of a painful struggle to reach. Hail slanted in sideways hitting Seth's long legs. The small cave shelter didn't offer much protection from the storm, but the cold air and wet boot had made his foot numb. He shivered and reached across to collect clean hailstones and put them into his plastic bottle. His water had run out when he'd used the last of it to swallow some painkillers. It was a horrendous storm, but he managed sleeping between bouts of thunder and lightning.

"I'm wet and cold and sore, Lord. What's the best thing for me to do now?"

No still small voice, or if it was there, Seth couldn't hear it. *I need to think logically. What would I tell someone else they should do?* He decided to wait for a break in the weather and then he'd get going again. He had to get off the ridge and his confidence in that decision was sound. A couple of hours later, he managed to find a sturdy stick to help steady himself and make slow, painful steps in the right direction.

Jessica looked at the clock again. It wasn't even ten minutes since she checked last time. Seth should've been home by now and she had his dinner warming in the oven. Maybe he felt he couldn't come home, or he didn't want to. Her heart broke. *It's okay Seth. We'll help you.*

"Auntie Jess, when's Dad coming back?"

Ryan had been quiet all day. He usually spent Saturdays shadowing his Dad on the farm.

"It's okay, Ry, your Dad will come home soon."

She wasn't sure about that, and it freaked her out. The kids needed a distraction from their worry. A bubble bath, a pillow fight and several bedtime stories seemed to work.

Maybe he was hurt. Her brother was an experienced climber and wouldn't take any risks. She knew that, but it was his state of mind that worried her. He might not be thinking clearly and that could cause a problem. Or, maybe he just needed another day to himself.

I think I'll wait until tomorrow before I begin to panic.

Jessica didn't sleep particularly well and spent half the night praying for Seth's safety. She woke to rain pattering on the tin roof. *Oh, great, that's all we need.* They went into Mt Barker to church. After the service, Jess explained it all to Reverend Bob.

"I had no idea Seth was adopted. No wonder he's having trouble working through it with everything else that's going on."

"I'm not sure what to do, Bob."

He understood Jessica's concern.

"Probably best to go home and check to see if he's arrived this morning. If he's not there, let me know and we'll get a search party together to find him."

Jess was relieved, a plan was in place. One she hoped they wouldn't need, but Seth wasn't home when they got back to the farm. She rang Bob.

He arranged for Todd, Liam and Keith to meet him at the caravan park. Bob had checked in at the Stirling Range National Park office on the way. The ranger was about to leave for a patrol, so they'd talked briefly in the rain to discover that Seth hadn't registered a climb on Friday. He drove down the road to the Stirling Range Caravan Park.

"Gazza," Bob knocked on the office door. He reached across and they shook hands.

"You're a bit early," Garry commented. "It's not wildflower season yet."

"No, just wondering if Seth was here last night. He was supposed to climb Bluff Knoll and camp here afterwards."

Bob's raincoat dripped on the floor.

"He hasn't been here as far as I know, but I'll give Rich a call. He's probably come in for afternoon tea at the farmhouse about now."

Garry shook his head.

"No, sorry. You look worried. Do you think Seth's missing?"

"Could be, we're not sure. I'm trying to cover all the bases before we go climbing around the mountain to look for him."

Worry lines appeared on Bob's usually calm face.

"There was a cracker of a storm up there late yesterday afternoon."

Bob sighed.

"That's not good news."

"Tell you what, if you need us, get the ranger to give us a ring and we'll come help."

"Thanks, Gazza, that's good of you."

Bob went out just as Liam, Todd and Keith pulled into the car park. It was still raining. They discussed their options but prayed first, seeking God's guidance and wisdom. Liam hadn't been to the Stirling Range before and even with the grey day found it beautiful.

"I'm not going to be much good here, guys, but I'll do whatever I can."

Todd had climbed Bluff Knoll many times since he was a child; Keith had climbed Mt Bruce and Joffre Gorge in the Karijini National Park up north. They pulled into the car park.

Seth's car wasn't there, and that raised more concerns.

"No point in climbing here, yet." Bob thought quickly. "Let's check the Mirlpunda Track and Gnowellen Road for his car first."

Surely he didn't attempt the Ridge Walk. Bob shook his head. The rain eased.

No vehicle at Mirlpunda. They drove along Sandalwood Road to Gnowellen Road and found his farm ute parked near the firebreak. Bob breathed a sigh of relief, at least he knew where to start now. They drove back to the Mirlpunda Track.

"Liam, you stay here and set up camp. I'll go back to the ranger and leave a message to let him know what we've found. Todd and Keith, study that map and get familiar with it. This is the obvious place for Seth to come out, he'd only planned one night away from home, so he might be hurt. I don't think he'll be lost because Seth knows the ridge really well. But, he was upset and we can't rule that out. Storms can confuse the best climbers, and Garry said there was a big one yesterday. He could be anywhere in there."

Bob didn't like the idea of going up that slippery slope to First Arrow. His age and size meant he'd be more of a liability than being helpful. Hopefully, the young fellows with the ranger might be able to manage it. *God help us,* he prayed.

The park ranger turned up twenty minutes after Bob got back. He had a survival kit and thermal blanket with his backpack of gear, and plenty of water.

"If we're going to get up there before dark, we'd better get going."

Todd and Keith were ready to leave, albeit, nervous about the whole idea. Neither of them understood Seth's decision to take on such a risky climb without letting anyone know what he was doing.

"I'll lead the way, and we need to keep an eye out for him. Seth could be 30 metres to either side of us and we could pass him without realising. The climb will be tough because it's wet but at least it's only drizzling now."

The men were pleased someone knew where they were going and what to do.

They set off in search of the missing man.

CHAPTER 17

Parishioners from the whole region were praying. Beryl had rung around with a prayer chain request for Seth's safety, and for the men going to find and rescue him. The light began to fade and Beryl's prayer was that Bob wouldn't be silly enough to climb that escape route at his age. It was difficult enough coming down, let alone trying to go up.

The tent provided shelter for Liam and Bob and they'd managed to rustle up some food and make billy tea. They had a fire built in half a 44-gallon drum with firewood that Garry and Rich had dropped off before dark. It didn't seem warranted to send anyone else up the hill when Bob was sure Seth would be in this particular area.

Liam felt useless, but he could pray. Seth had become a good friend since they'd met six months ago and they'd shared many personal stories. He was afraid for his friend and felt that he'd let him down.

"I should've been more supportive." Liam muttered to himself.

"What was that?" Bob asked.

"Oh, sorry, I was thinking out loud. I should've made myself more available for Seth. He's been going through a pretty bad time. I can't believe he'd attempt something like this on his own."

Bob reached over and patted Liam on the shoulder, nearly knocking him off his camp stool. *I didn't realise he had such big hands,* Liam thought, but kept it to himself this time.

"Don't beat yourself up, lad. We men do what we have to in our own way and climbing calms Seth. That's why he's up there, and I think you'll find something went wrong. I hope he'll be okay. We just need to keep praying that it isn't serious and they'll get back down safely."

Liam nodded and went quiet again.

It rained heavier for about twenty minutes, and headlights flashed into the tent as two vehicles pulled up beside their camp. Four people piled out of the cars with cameras and tripods and lights – looking for some action.

"Reporters," Bob groaned. "Now it'll be all over the news."

Bob and Liam were questioned but gave careful answers not wanting to stir up a hornet's nest. Seth's state of mind was none of their business.

Another tent popped up, and a cameraman walked partway up the track zooming his lens in for any sight of the rescue mission returning.

"They'll stay up there until first light," Bob told them. "It's too dangerous to climb down in the dark. Might as well get a bit of shut-eye."

He and Liam lay down on their bedrolls and slept for a few hours. The news crew stood around the fire and kept it stoked up. They weren't going to sleep, the old fellow might be wrong and they didn't want to miss anything.

"Coffee?" Bob asked Liam when he stirred awake.

"Yes, please."

Liam was stiff and cold even though he'd been in a sleeping bag. At around seven o'clock in the morning, a tinge of light began to emerge in the east. The rain had stopped, and Bob thought it wouldn't be too long before they would return. The tension in the camp with reporters calling out to each other while using binoculars and zoom lenses to focus on the track entrance and the mountain was annoying. Liam wished they'd go away and leave them alone. Seth wouldn't want them in his face when they finally made it down.

At 9.00am one of the crew shouted and everyone became alert.

"I can see them, here they come."

At about half a kilometre up the slope the returning men could just be seen coming over a mound. The cameraman scrambled as far as he could among rocks and undergrowth with his equipment balanced on his shoulder. He wanted to capture the arrival scene as it unfolded.

The park ranger came down first. Seth followed leaning heavily on Todd and Keith for support to manage the steep and challenging descent. He had the thermal blanket tied around him and looked pale and in pain. They were all damp and tired but in good spirits.

"What happened up there?"

"How did you get hurt?"

"Why were you out there in this weather?"

A barrage of questions aimed at the injured man put them all on the back foot.

"Hang on a minute, you guys," the ranger interrupted, "let's get this fellow sorted out a bit first and then you can speak to him."

His authority was respected and they backed off.

"Hi," Liam approached his friend and hugged him.

"Hi. Thanks for coming."

"I haven't done much, not like these guys."

Liam indicated toward Todd and Keith and the ranger.

"You're here, though."

"Yep."

A fold-up camp chair was opened out and Seth almost fell into it. Bob gave him a warm cup of tea with two sugars, just how he liked it. His older friend rubbed his big palm over Seth's head.

"I'm glad they found you."

He passed him a bowl of oatmeal and milk with a spoon.

"Thanks, I don't think I'd have made it down by now without help. I would've been hours away yet."

A camp stool was placed in front of him.

"Let's put that sprained ankle up," the ranger instructed. "And you can have some more Panadol after you've eaten your breakfast."

The ranger had removed Seth's boot, checked for circulation and bruising and taped and bandaged his ankle when they'd found him up the track during the night. His jeans were cut to release the pressure on the swelling of his ankle, and he'd slept with his foot raised on a rock with a blanket to prop it up. The newsmen interviewed Seth, filming him as they did before they packed up and dashed off to report their story. The remaining men thanked the ranger for his help and then stood in prayerful thanks before heading off to the hospital in Mt Barker.

The doctor insisted that Seth stay at least overnight. He had suffered hypothermia, was dehydrated and needed an x-ray of his ankle to check for fractures. Warm drinks and the gradual heating of his body was monitored. His fluid intake and output was measured. All a lot of fuss in Seth's opinion but Jessica would not allow him to ignore the medical advice they'd been given. Her brother wanted to go home and curl up in his own bed, but it had to wait. At least he hadn't been seriously injured; she reminded him that it could've been much worse.

Ryan and Alicia wanted to see their Dad after a trying day waiting for news about him. Auntie Jess said they had to go to school, even though they didn't want to.

"Dad," Alicia ran into the hospital room and jumped up beside him on the bed.

She kissed and hugged him over and over again even though his prickly stubble left a rash on her soft skin. Ryan stood by him and held his hand.

"Dad, you should've seen Leesh today."

"Why, Ry, what did she do this time?"

"She stood up for me, big time."

"Really?"

That didn't surprise Seth.

"Tell me what happened."

Ryan explained how a couple of the boys in his class were bullying him because he didn't want to go and play footie. They called him a sissy and Alicia was furious when she heard the sing-song 'Ryan is a sissy, Ryan is a sissy.' She'd stormed over and told them off.

"She yelled at them, Dad, telling them they'd be upset if it were their Dad missing on the mountain. They looked scared, and then they said - 'sorry, we didn't know it was your Dad they're looking for.' They were surprised it was you."

"Yes, it is. So you better stop being nasty right now." Ryan mimicked his sister voice and stance with hands on hips, eyes squinted and lips pursed. He laughed at the memory.

"She looked like she might bop them. They ran off to play and left me alone."

Seth and Jessica swapped an amused glance.

Ryan was so proud of her.

"Then I sat with Ry outside his classroom, Dad. I didn't feel like playing anymore, either. That's when the teacher came and told us you'd been found. We're so glad you're back."

Alicia snuggled in as close as she could get to her father. He reassured them he was going to be okay.

"We had a pillow fight," Ryan was the chatty one for a change.

"I bet that was Auntie Jessica's idea."

"Yeah. How did you know?"

"She liked a good pillow fight or two when she was growing up. I always won, though."

"Come on, you two. I think it's time to go home now."

"You don't want to go there, Tati?"

Jess was moved by his endearment and felt a sense of healing wash over her. She leaned across and kissed Seth on the cheek.

"I love you, Seth Tawnya Jarvis."

In that moment it occurred to Seth that, yes, that is who he was and he was okay with it. The kids hugged him and said goodbye. Bob walked in as they went to leave.

"How're you feeling now?"

The older man took a seat beside the hospital bed.

"Yeah, much better. Thanks. Still sore and tired, though."

"You'll be right in a day or two."

Seth nodded. A knock on the door revealed Todd with Millie alongside him when they opened it.

"Is it all right for us to come in? We just saw Jessica leaving with Ryan and Alicia."

"Sure is."

The pair stood beside the bed, neither sat. A nurse came to take Seth's temperature and blood pressure. She checked his water jug and wrote on the chart at the end of the bed, then spoke to the visitors.

"I think it would be good for Seth to get some rest. He's had a stream of people through here in the last couple of hours."

They acknowledged her subtle suggestion to leave soon and agreed they wouldn't linger.

"Well, if I thought no-one cared about me, I was wrong." Seth shrugged his shoulders.

"That was never the case, young man." Bob reassured him.

They chatted for a bit and then Bob decided to go, he sensed something was afoot and didn't want to intrude.

"I'll see you tomorrow." He waved and left the room.

An awkward silence hovered over them.

"What's up?" Seth wanted to know.

Todd took Millie's hand.

"What are you doing?" she asked him.

"The vision, Millie, remember the dream."

"Oh, yes. If you think so."

"Vision? What's that all about?"

Seth was slightly bemused by Todd's obscure secrecy.

"You're not going to faint, are you?"

Seth laughed, remembering Millie's collapse when he first met her.

"No, but you might. So it's just as well you're already laying down."

Todd placed Millie's hand over Seth's pale bruised and scratched one resting on the bed.

"Seth, meet your mother."

Seth looked at Millie, then Todd and back to Millie again.

"Millicent Elizabeth Glen … something?"

"Glendalow. Yes, that was me."

Todd left the room wiping the moisture from the corner of his eyes.

Millie held Seth's hand in her own.

"Hello, son."

"You're my birth-mother?"

"Yes, I am. Can you ever forgive me for letting you go?"

Seth shook his head in disbelief. Millie's joy was nearly washed away, thinking the movement meant he couldn't forgive her.

"I never knew I was adopted. My parents, well, my adoptive parents never told me."

Millie wanted to withdraw her hand, her heart was heavy.

"Did you want to give me away?"

"No, no! I never would have. I wanted you more than anything. They took you away and left me empty-handed. Seth, there has never been a day since you were born that I haven't thought about you. I've wondered where you were, if you were happy and whether or not you were in a good family."

"Then there's nothing to forgive, but I want to know more. Soon, if you don't mind?"

Seth smiled, a healthy glow softened his weather-beaten features and he rubbed his climb-roughened thumb over the back of Millie's hand. Her relief was palpable.

"Mind? Never, it'll be a privilege. I want you to know I've always loved you, son, always."

They both had tears slipping down their cheeks.

Millie pulled a framed photograph out of her carry bag and passed it to Seth.

"This is your father. His name was Harold John Lockridge, and he'd want me to tell you that he loved you, too."

Seth took the picture and was surprised at what he saw.

"My eyes. I get my eyes from him?"

"Yes, you do. You're like Harold in many ways, Seth. That's why I reacted like I did when I first met you. It was such a shock."

The lump in Seth's throat wouldn't allow him to voice any more words.

They embraced, and he swallowed hard.

"I never knew," he whispered.

CHAPTER 18

A red crepe-paper carpet greeted Seth at the front door. His fans cheered him on as he swaggered along with his head held high in the air. Jessica had hinted at the surprise waiting for him at home.

"We saw you on TV, Dad."

"I am the star," he said with a plum-in-the-mouth accent.

Alicia jumped up and down while clapping her hands, and Ryan yelled a loud woo-hoo.

"Thank you, thank you."

Seth made a bow and the children ran off giggling.

"You looked awful, Seth, but the kids didn't notice. They were too excited to see you on the screen."

"The reporters didn't capture my best side."

"What best side? You could use a shave. There's more than a five o'clock shadow on that chin." He'd seen the short report on the local news station, too, but wasn't worried about how he looked. "I might keep the mo," he laughed.

Jessica enjoyed the fun they'd had with the kids. It was good to have some lightheartedness back in the house.

"Cup of tea?" she asked.

"Yes, please. Tea never tastes as good in the hospital, does it?"

Jess smiled.

"I hadn't noticed but that's because I've been doing it for years."

He nodded.

"Of course. I didn't think about that."

"Speaking of which, I'm on duty tomorrow night. I'll have to leave early tomorrow morning. Will you be all right if I go?"

Seth exaggerated limping to the table with a pained look on his face.

"Oh, we'll manage," his light green eyes twinkled with mischief.

Jessica ignored the teasing.

"I've wanted to tell you I've applied for a nursing position in Albany."

Surprise showed on Seth's face.

"That's great. We might get to see more of you. When did you do that?"

"A few months ago. I'm sick of living in the city and all the hustle and bustle every day. I was a bit worried you might be upset about me leaving the apartment."

"Don't be, it's fine. We'll hang onto it for a while. You never know, the kids might want to go to university one day. We can always rent it out before then, and it can earn us a bit of money."

"Thanks. I feel better about that now. I'll be back on the weekend 'cos I've got a date on Saturday night."

Seth's eyes widened and he physically sat up straight.

"Wow. Who's taking you out?"

"Not telling, yet."

"Spoilsport."

She grinned. Seth saw the prospect of the date light up her face. Jessica's beauty came from within he realised. Her face had a feminine handsomeness he supposed, but it was her compassionate and caring demeanour that people noticed. *Who was it?* His curiosity was piqued.

"It's my turn to change the subject now. Why don't you revamp the house? It's still the same as when we were kids."

"I don't mind, and Felicity never showed any interest in it. Her shopping sprees to David Jones in Albany on Saturday's were for clothes and make-up. We're still using the stash of black and white houndstooth plastic shopping bags."

Jessica shook her head.

"Well, it wouldn't hurt you to at least think about painting the walls. I'm happy to help pick colours."

"I'll give it some thought. You're probably right."

"I usually am." At that comment she shifted aside just in time to miss the expected playful hit coming her way.

Felicity's letter sat open on Seth's desk. He'd forgotten how rationalised and explicit her words had been. It showed little emotion and sounded like a clear-cut school report.

Seth,

I'm leaving and by the time you find this, I will have already gone. The bus leaves from town soon and I'll be on it. I will drop the keys for the car into the General Store and you can collect them from there. You'll need to pick Alicia up from Kindy at 2.30pm and Ryan from his classroom at 3.00pm. If you can't manage it, I'm sure your parents would do it for you.

Please do not try and contact me or come looking for me. It's over. I will not be coming back. Ever. This life is not what I wanted and I can't live a lie anymore. It sounds selfish, and maybe it is, but I will go mad with frustration if I stay.

I foolishly got caught up in the romance and youthful fun of the moment. It all happened too fast and didn't give me time to consider the consequences. My ambition for a significant role in education can never be achieved here. I thought I could do this country life, wife, mother, family thing but I'm deceiving myself, and you and the children.

It is best I go. I know Ryan and Alicia have a better chance of being happy living with you and all the good things you offer them. Your love, security and stability are what they need. I am becoming bitter and resentful. The children will grow up knowing rejection from me because the responsibility of their care would continue to thwart the desires of my heart.

I love teaching students, watching them learn and increase their knowledge. But I don't have any other responsibility toward them and at the end of the day they go home to their families. I can't stand the mundane life of meals and bath time and washing, ironing and cleaning. It's not what I want and it's destroying the me that I want to be.

I'd like to say I'm sorry, but I'd be lying. I am not sorry, I need to do this and have decided the time is now.

You will recover from the shock and the children will be fine. They will grow into kind, healthy and well-balanced adults under your care. They should be released from the damage I'd do if I continue on this soul-destroying path. Don't blame yourself. It is not your fault.

Felicity

Seth was stunned. At the time, the hurt and pain of his wife leaving had blinded him to the absolute truth. Felicity painted a clear picture of despising domesticity and all that went with their lifestyle. For the first time, he recognised how damaging it would've been if she had stayed.

So why the shift in attitude now? Oliver. It had to be Oliver.

He faxed the letter to his lawyer asking for advice on the next steps to take in the process. Seth didn't want it to get ugly for the children's sake, and his prayer was that an amicable agreement out of court could be achieved sooner rather than later.

An afternoon tea banquet was set out on the table at Millie's house. She'd baked biscuits and fresh scones with home-made strawberry jam and whipped cream. They were on pretty plates and she'd used her best lace tablecloth. The children's eyes nearly popped out of their heads when they saw it all.

"Yum," Alicia couldn't wait to have some.

"Remember your manners, Leesh."

Seth had reminded them before they left home to be on their best behaviour. Millie had invited them during the week to come on Saturday afternoon. The plan was to get to know each other and use the opportunity to ask questions. Some of them might be hard to answer, but they were both prepared for that. Taking the children with him wasn't easy in Seth's opinion. He didn't know how he'd manage them and have a personal conversation in their company. He need not have worried.

"Tea?" Millie enquired after Seth.

"Yes, please."

"Milk?"

He nodded. She poured two white teas and passed him his drink and the sugar bowl. Seth put two teaspoons into his cup and stirred it vigorously. Millie smiled.

"I see you may have a sweet tooth like me."

Two teaspoons of sugar went into her teacup and she stirred it well. They chuckled at the idea of it.

"Maybe that's where Alicia gets it from. She loves dessert."

Seth and Millie appreciated the humour of the moment when they saw a scone and a biscuit with a bite out of it on Alicia's plate.

"I don't mind a bit of cake myself," Millie commented.

Soon after, Millie produced a parcel for the children with new colouring books, textas, and stickers for them to amuse themselves. A basket of books and toys nearby was available for them to play with and read. They sat at the end of the table engrossed in what they were doing without noticing the quiet conversation between the adults.

"It's a bit difficult to know where to start," Millie's brow creased as she spoke.

"I've had a couple of questions going around in my head for days. Maybe I could ask you those?" Seth offered.

"That's a good idea. Fire away."

Millie's heart was racing and she felt a twinge of nerves. *Please, Lord, don't let me say anything that will hurt my boy even more.* She took a deep breath and waited. Seth looked up at the ceiling and back down to the table. He was as nervous as Millie.

"Well, you said you were left 'empty-handed' when I was born. Aren't babies given up for adoption taken away before the mother sees the child?"

A silent shudder ran through Millie at the memory of it.

"Yes, they do, but God blessed me with a very brief hold of you. The matron told the young trainee midwife to take the baby to the nursery when she left to get some forgotten paperwork. The girl took you out of the bassinet, and as she turned she knocked a tray of instruments on the floor. In her panic she handed you to me and said, 'here, hold him for a minute.' While she was collecting the mess off the floor, the matron returned and saw me caressing your face and kissing your forehead."

Millie held her arms together like cradling a babe as she spoke, a light shone in her eyes.

"She yelled at the poor girl. 'Nurse! What do you think you're doing?' Then Matron rushed over and pulled you out of my arms, leaving me shattered. But I'd had the chance to look at you, touch you and I knew you were a boy. I praise God for that cherished moment."

Tears filled her eyes. She swallowed hard and played with the corner of her handkerchief. Seth exhaled a deep breath slowly while he braced for more.

"So, you didn't want to give me away. How come you had to?"

"I was very young. Harold and me, we were in love and made a mistake. We would've married with my parent's permission but that didn't happen. Harold was forbidden to see me ever again. He'd tainted my 'reputation' in my mother and father's opinion. After I came home from the hospital, I found my room scoured of anything to do with Harold. Photographs, gifts and letters had been removed and the pain of it added to my already broken heart. Dare I tell you? I hated my parents at the time for all of that."

"I think it's understandable you would feel that way after what they'd put you through."

"But they didn't know Harold had left a letter for me at the hospital. He said to look in the space between the picket fence and the gatepost for notes. He'd get someone to hide them there for him. We did that for years. I'd collect the house mail and bend down to pull a weed and find his note, and put one in it for him. I found it quite amusing when people with a dog, or on a bike, or with a pram would walk past and make excuses to bend down and make the switch right beside our letterbox."

"Huh, that was clever."

"It's all that kept me sane. We waited to elope when I was 21, and on my birthday I left home and never went back."

"Did you have other children? Do I have any brothers or sisters?"

"Sadly, no, we had many miscarriages."

Her voice was only a whisper.

"I guess I'm it then," Seth's tender smile tugged at Millie's heart.

Thank you, Lord, I am blessed beyond belief.

"You are, and I am glad of it."

CHAPTER 19

Liam and Courtney insisted Seth stay over at Lancaster Guest House for the night. Seth's foot ached and he needed to put it up with an ice-pack to relieve the pain. He agreed, and the children were beside themselves. They loved staying at Courtney's place. They helped to cook dinner, set the table and played UNO with Liam and their father.

Courtney served coffee after the children had gone to bed. The adults chewed over the whole rescue event.

"I need to tell you something."

Seth caught his hosts' attention immediately.

"Millie is my birth mother."

"What? No way."

"Wow, how weird is that?"

"Yeah, and I'm just like her husband, Harold. He was my father and we have the same eyes, same build, same walk."

Courtney was stunned.

"No wonder she fainted when she met you."

Seth nodded.

"It was a shock to her. She never expected she would get to meet me. Millie's kept quiet about it since Bob's birthday party and didn't know whether or not to say anything to me. Todd was the only other person who knew."

"Todd told me he was good at keeping secrets." Courtney remembered one of their earlier conversations not long after she first met him.

Millie had shared Todd's vision with Seth and what it meant. He told his friends about it. They were moved to see how God's hand had been at work. Courtney stood to clear away the cups.

"It's a relief to share this with you. What's the saying? 'A burden shared is a burden halved.' I think it's right, too."

Seth retired early and felt the soothing comfort of real friends.

The lawyer rang. Seth was disturbed by the conversation but decided to give himself time to work through it. He didn't want to get angry again. Felicity's demands were still unreasonable.

Communication from the lawyer recommended Family Dispute Resolution for their parenting roles and to make amicable arrangements to avoid court action. The best result for the children should be the priority.

It all sounded complicated to Seth. He wanted his kids lives to remain normal. He'd prayed for what was right for them, and if it meant sharing custody, he had to trust it was for the children's benefit.

Felicity's solicitor had sent a Notice of Claim requesting Ryan and Alicia spend all school holidays and long weekends with her including the Christmas and Easter breaks.

"Whew, that's a big ask."

Jessica sat across from Seth at the dining room table. He rested his head in his hands.

"That means I won't have them during any downtime. It will be all routine days, and in the busy seasons on the farm I'll only have a little bit of time for them. It's not fair. Felicity doesn't even know them anymore."

"What about the letter, Seth?"

"I sent it, but my lawyer doesn't want to use it unless we have to muscle our way through this."

"It needs muscle." Jessica didn't make light of it. "Use it, Seth. It seems Oliver is the one directing the action here, not Felicity. I doubt she has given thought to all the work that comes with those visits. Her idea will be picnics, movies and trips to the zoo and museums. The novelty will wear off quickly."

Seth looked at his sister. She was right.

"Okay. I'll ask the lawyer to send it."

He went to his study and put together a proposal he thought was fair. One with a counter-offer of short term visits until they got to know each other. Ryan would never cope with a stretch of two weeks at a time. Not yet.

Jessica had the gas oven going and managed to prepare the vegetables on the narrow well-worn kitchen benches. She'd become used to her newer appliances and spacious kitchen in her flat and this all seemed very tired by comparison. *At least it's not the old wood-fired Metters No. 2,* she thought thankfully. Their father had revamped the kitchen from the original one in the early 1960's but it had remained the same ever since.

"Dinner's ready," Jess called.

Seth had sat at his desk oblivious to the time and didn't realise it was that late. They enjoyed roast beef and vegetables. Jessica ran a bubble bath for the kids and they were tucked in for the night.

"You spoil them," Seth wagged a finger at her.

"Auntie's privilege," she smiled back.

"I 'spose. They do love you."

"And I love them."

"So how was the date?"

"Nice."

Seth took a step back.

"Nice. What sort of a word is that?"

"Non-commital."

"Oh, so the date-ee isn't going to get a commitment from you?"

Seth looked concerned.

"I didn't say that."

"What did you mean then?"

"That I'm not telling you any details. It was more than nice if you must know."

He smiled a cheeky grin.

"Good."

"Good. What sort of a word is that?"

"Non-commital!"

"Ha, ha."

They embraced. Seth hoped she wouldn't end up hurt. After his own experience, he wouldn't wish it on anyone. Jessica deserved a happily ever after kind of love.

The phone rang at 9.00pm. Seth was worried that something was wrong when a phone call came that late in the evening.

"Seth."

"Felicity?"

Her voice sounded strange.

"Yes, it's me. I got the letter today, and I'm upset with myself."

He hoped that was a good thing to hear.

"Why is that, Felicity?"

A quiet pause ensued.

"I'd forgotten I said all those things. I'm sorry, really, I am."

"What are you sorry for? Writing the letter? Or that you wrote harsh words and meant them?"

Why now; because it's being used as evidence against you?

"All of it."

He went quiet.

"Are you still there, Seth?"

"Yes, I'm here."

"It was wrong to expect you to give up Ryan and Alicia for all the holidays."

Please, Lord, help us to sort this out, Seth prayed.

"Can we agree on a few short visits, so the kids get to know you, and Oliver?"

"Yes, I think that's best. It's not what Oliver has been encouraging me to do. He thinks I've cheated myself of the relationships I should have with my children. And, I daresay, he is right. But ..." she drew a deep breath ... "I've realised that I'm still that person, the one in the letter. Oliver can't be the one to decide what I do about this. It has to be between you and me."

Seth let relief flood through him.

Thank you, Lord.

"You have no idea how much that pleases me, Felicity. I can bring the kids to Perth on the long-weekend in September for a visit if you like. We can come up on Friday night and be available on Saturday or Sunday – whatever suits you. Just for an hour or two."

That'll give me a few weeks to prepare them for it. All that way for such a short time, but I have to make an effort to make this work.

"Okay, I'll let you know which day we choose closer to the time. I knew you'd have the best solution to all of this."

That's encouraging, he thought.

"We'll work it out."

"Bye, Seth, and thanks."

He hung up and breathed a sigh of relief.

CHAPTER 20

Ryan's urgent plea made Seth rush outdoors. He was crouched down in the corner of the verandah between the wall and the barbeque.

"Dad! Come quick. I think Mallee's having her puppies. She's panting a lot. I saw her scratching around and she wouldn't sit still. Now she's done a big yellow wee and some sticky stuff's come out."

Seth saw the dog begin to strain with a contraction. He could barely reach her to feel how far along she was in her labour. The first puppy was delivered soon after.

"Oh, yuck. Mallee ate that horrible stuff around the puppy." Ryan hadn't seen a litter birthed before.

"That's what they do, Ry. Look, it's healthy and it's a boy."

Alicia didn't want to watch the birthing process. Ryan was entranced, even with Mallee displaying her natural animal instincts. Four hours later five wriggly red and tan Kelpie pups were nursing at their mother's side.

"Aw, they're so cute."

Alicia returned after all the action was over.

"Three boys and two girls," Seth patted his dog. "You've done well little mother."

"Which one will we give to Courtney?"

Alicia wanted to know straight away.

"We'll wait a little while and see what their personalities are like."

"I didn't know dogs had persa ... persnal ..." she endeavoured to say the word.

"Personalities," Seth re-iterated, smiling at her fumbled attempts. "Yes, they do and we'll find one with just the right traits to give Courtney. Let's leave Mallee to take care of them now and we'll check later to make sure they're okay."

Seth planned to keep one of the dogs to train alongside Mallee in the paddock. Courtney could have one and the others would be sold to farmers who knew of the excellent qualities of his sheep dog and the male breeder he used.

Four weeks later they were weaned and growing into playful, chubby puppies. Ryan had taken the feeding and care of them seriously. Alicia would play with them for a while but soon tire of it. Seth could see that Ryan would be consistent with training the dogs under his guidance in the coming weeks.

"Ry, I need to talk to you about going to visit your Mum on Saturday."

His son's face fell. They'd had this discussion several times.

"Do we have to go, Dad?"

"Yes, you do. It's only going to be for a couple of hours."

Tears welled in Ryan's eyes and he shook his head.

"I don't want to do it, let Alicia go by herself. She wants to see her."

"I can't let that happen. I'm sorry, but you have to give this a try."

"I don't have a choice, do I?"

"No, but I promise we'll watch the footy final in the afternoon together. Auntie Jess has a big TV and she'll be there with us, you know how excited she gets watching football. Collingwood is playing against Carlton for the premiership."

Ryan knew his auntie's favourite team was Collingwood. It would be a great game.

"Okay."

The boy's shoulders slumped in resignation. It broke Seth's heart to see his son struggle with this. He shouldn't have to be forced into it, but Ryan had to learn that sometimes we have to do difficult things in life. If it upset him too much, Seth would have to speak to Felicity about it. Ryan's welfare was important and developing a new relationship with his mother is what mattered. It would be different, and Seth suspected that's what worried his son. He probably feared being rejected again. Seth prayed and kept praying that this visit wouldn't hurt his children.

Their neighbours, Fred and Eunice, promised to take care of Mallee and the puppies while they were in Perth. Alicia was pleased about going to the city but Ryan sat quietly staring out the window as they drove up the highway. Seth's heart was heavy for him. When they arrived in Perth at dinnertime, Seth pulled into a Hungry Jack's car park.

"Are we getting a burger?"

They were Ryan's first words since they'd left home and a lightness shone in his eyes. It pleased Seth.

"Yep, and you can have whatever you want."

"Yum. I want a Whopper with coke and chips, please."

The threesome ordered and ate their meals inside the restaurant. The children went into the playground while Seth drank his coffee and watched from his seat. *Oh, Lord, I feel sick about this whole thing. Please, please Father God, watch over Ryan and Alicia. I pray that Felicity - and Oliver - will have wisdom in how they treat them.* Seth had committed them into God's care but it didn't take away the feeling in the pit of his stomach.

At bedtime, Seth gave Ryan a gift.

"Dad," his eyes widened. "A camera for me?"

"Yes, and tomorrow when you go to the park you can take photos of the wildflowers."

"Like you do."

"Almost, this camera doesn't do close-ups like my big one but I think you'll have fun with it. Stay back a bit and the photos will be in focus."

"Thanks, Dad."

Ryan hugged his father and whispered 'I love you' in his ear.

"Let Alicia have a few turns, too. Don't get annoyed with her. There's a 24-shot film in there, and when you've used it all, you won't be able to take any more photos. I'll show you how to rewind the film into the canister before we take it out later."

"Leesh, this is for you."

He gave her a pink shoulder bag with a purse and some money in it. She put it on and wore it to bed. Seth rolled his eyes.

In the morning the children had showers and dressed in their best clothes and shoes. Jessica brushed Alicia's hair and clipped it back with pretty slides. Ryan looked pale. They prayed together before they got into the car to go to Kings Park Botanical Gardens. The arrangement was to meet by the Floral Clock at 9.00am. Felicity had said they would provide a picnic morning tea and walk through the wildflower displays. Seth could collect them from the same place two hours later.

Waiting was awkward. Seth distracted the children by talking about the big garden clock where the grey bushes were trimmed to look like Roman numerals and explained how the large white hands told the time like a real clock. They liked the replica of a small Swiss chalet surrounded by pansies and petunias. Just as the big hand reached the number XII at the top, Felicity and Oliver arrived.

Felicity wore navy slacks with a white cotton crochet twin set, and carried a basket covered with a cloth. Oliver was dressed in black trousers with a lemon coloured polo shirt and a black leather jacket. He had a picnic rug over his arm. Seth felt shabby by comparison to them in his jeans and fleecy check shirt.

"Hello," Felicity greeted them.

She kept biting her bottom lip as she spoke to the children and introduced them to Oliver. Seth recognised the nervous habit and thought it was a good sign. Maybe it will turn out okay. She's not plunging into this over-confident. He hugged the kids, told them to have a nice time and gestured taking a photo to Ryan. His son gave a weak smile but it was a smile, nevertheless. Seth turned and walked away, tears stinging his eyes. *Trust me, I'll take care of them.* That still, small voice echoed in his head. *Okay, Lord, I trust you.*

Two hours felt like an eternity, but 11.00am came around and Seth was at the garden clock again. He'd driven around the city, stopped for a coffee at a cafe and then wandered around in a few shops not looking at anything in particular. His heart was pounding, along with the headache behind his eyes. *I do trust you, Lord, but I can't pretend I'm not worried.*

Alicia came bouncing up the path holding Felicity's hand with Ryan a pace or two behind his sister. Oliver wasn't with them. Seth blew out a breath and put a smile on his face.

"Hi, did you have a nice time?"

He asked the polite question.

"It's not what I expected."

Felicity gave the reply he thought he would hear.

"Dad, we took lots of photo's on Ryan's Instamatic camera. That's what Oliver said it is called. I practised saying it until I got it right, in-sta-mat-ic, insta-matic." She smiled, pleased at her achievement. "And I got an ice-cream with my money. I bought one for Ry, too. Felicity and Oliver didn't want one."

"That's good, honey."

A car pulled up at the kerb and tooted. Felicity said goodbye and retreated to the vehicle. Everyone waved as they drove away. *Thank goodness that's over.* Both parents thought the same thing at the same time.

"How were the wildflowers?" Seth asked from genuine interest and not just to pump them for details of the time they spent away from him.

"There were heaps of everlastings, Dad."

"Yeah, and they're called carpets," Alicia added. "I thought that was a bit funny, 'cos we weren't allowed to walk on them. There were pink and white ones, and they can be called paper daisies, too. If you hang them upside down when you cut them they'll dry and you can keep them forever. That's how come they get to be called everlastings."

Seth smiled at Alicia's exuberance about what she had learned this morning.

"I loved the dark green and red Kangaroo Paws." Ryan held up his camera, "I took some photos to show you."

"And there were some yellow button flowers, too. I can't remember the name of them."

They chatted about the massive jarrah tree trunk that had been cut down a long time ago and how they'd tried to count the growth rings but couldn't. There were too many of them.

It seemed the children had managed the visit quite well from what Seth could understand. There was a pause in the conversation and then Ryan spoke.

"Dad, Leesh asked Felicity, or Mum, I don't know what to call her," he paused.

"You'll work it out, Ry. What did Alicia ask?"

"Why she doesn't want to live with us. It was a bit embarrassing and Mum didn't know what to say. Then ..."

"Ryan, are you telling tales here?"

His son looked confused.

"I don't think so, Dad. It's just what happened while they were talking by the pond where there's a statue of a lady holding a baby."

"It's called the Pioneer Women's Memorial, Ry." Alicia corrected him, and then continued, "I asked her why she liked Oliver instead of you, Dad. You're much nicer and better looking, too."

This from a six-year-old. Seth cringed, he should have known Leesh would do as much. *Oh, well, out of the mouth's of babes* – as they say … but he would have to address it - just another thing to have to deal with. And there he'd been thinking it had gone well.

"When does the footy final start, Dad?" Ryan wanted to know.

This was the fifth year the Aussie rules football final was televised live even though it was a delayed telecast in Western Australia. That's why Seth hadn't turned the radio on. He wanted to enjoy the game without knowing the outcome beforehand.

"The game hasn't started yet, and we'll be back in plenty of time. Auntie Jess is going to have some lunch ready for us when we get to the apartment."

"Good. I'm hungry."

"I thought you had morning tea and an ice-cream already."

"Only the ice-cream, I felt sick before and couldn't eat any of the fancy stuff Mum, um, Felicity had for us."

Ryan's confusion over what to call his mother was a problem but Seth didn't want to think about how they would confront that today.

They parked the car and went to the front door of the apartment. Seth could hear talking inside, and it wasn't just the television. He heard Jessica and a man's voice that sounded familiar. He unlocked the door but knocked as they went through thinking they might need some warning that they'd arrived.

Keith jumped up from the couch to greet him looking very pleased with himself. Seth's surprise was evident.

"So, do I know who the someone is now? That is assuming you're here to see Jess, not me."

Keith grinned at him.

"Yes, my friend, I'm here to see your sister."

"Well, well …," Seth shook his head in wonder.

It was the last thing he was expecting today.

CHAPTER 21

Jessica had invited Keith to come and watch the game with them to ease the shift from being Seth's friend to joining the family circle. The pair held hands, shared the occasional kiss and looked doe-eyed at each other throughout the football game.

There were shouts of advice for the players and yells of delight when Collingwood got a goal. It had been raining in Melbourne and the ground was slippery and muddy. Collingwood had won the previous two grand finals and Jess was fired up for her team to have a third win in a row. Carlton were up by a single point at half-time, and the game had been hard fought by both teams.

"Yes, yes, yes. Another one. That's five more goals now. We're gonna do it," Jess yelled. Alicia and Ryan were right there with their aunt, shaking fists and yelling out.

"Keep the pressure on."

Groans were expelled when classic marks were taken by the opposition and the game swung in Carlton's favour again. Neither team would give up and the battle was on. The premiership team had finished on top of the ladder and been undefeated in the finals. Jess rested her head on Keith's shoulder for comfort when the whistle blew and Carlton had beaten Collingwood by twenty points. She hated to admit they had deserved the win. They watched the cup presentation, and the naming of best player on ground for the Norm Smith Medal won by Bruce Douall. The broadcast concluded when the winning team ran a lap of honour around the Melbourne Cricket Ground.

There was a quiet interlude as the noise of the crowd's cheering stopped when they turned the television off. Jessica looked at her brother, who was giving her the eye.

"Are one of you going to let me in on the details?" Seth asked in trepidation. He didn't want to invade their privacy but he was curious about how it all came about.

"Sure," Keith replied. "Jess can tell you if she's got any voice left."

He laughed and enjoyed putting her on the spot.

"Well," she nudged Keith, who sat close to her while Alicia slept on her knee. "We met at Courtney's birthday party. Remember? I came to the farm because I was worried about you and all the stuff going on with Felicity."

"Yeah, and you weren't invited but Liam said you could come. So what happened? I thought you and Todd had hit it off."

"Ah. No. Todd and I are just friends. I'm older and much too serious for him."

The men laughed.

"What? I'm not mature. Is that what you think?"

"No. But you make it sound like you're ancient."

"Keith is the ancient one. He's already forty, old like you."

"And you'll be thirty next year. That's a pretty big gap, eleven years. I reckon there's only a couple of years difference between you and Todd. You two are a lot closer in age."

"You're missing the point here, Seth."

"What point is that, Keith?"

"We've fallen in love."

Keith declared the news while looking deep into Jessica's eyes and squeezing her hand.

"At the party? Love at first sight?" Seth asked while shaking his head in disbelief.

"Not really. We had a great chat and Keith asked if he could have my phone number. He's been ringing me ever since. We got to know each other through our conversations."

"Okay, and then you went on a date."

Seth remembered the non-commital quips they'd shared.

"Or two, or three and now whenever Jess has time off I come to Perth, or she comes down to the vineyard. Don't panic. She stays at Annie and Tom O'Reilly's place."

"They never said anything about it."

Keith looked at his friend with a grin.

"Sworn to secrecy. I am their boss, you know. Annie has savoured the romance of it all. She keeps reminding Tom about their 'courtship' as she calls it, but he's not getting the hint. Water off a duck's back."

Seth laughed.

"And," Jess added. "I got the job at Albany Regional Hospital. I start in a few weeks."

"That's great. Where will you live?"

"I've got accommodation at the Nurses' Quarters. It'll only take a two-minute walk to go to and from work. No more sitting in the car on the road for an hour or longer, trying to find a parking bay when I get there or feeling unsafe walking around in the dark. I'm looking forward to it."

Seth thought about it for a minute.

"I'm happy for you. Both of you."

Seth shifted his arm from around Ryan's sleeping body.

"So is Vicki," Keith added.

"She's been nagging at me for years to get a girlfriend."

Alarmed by the statement, Seth's thoughts set him on the verge of panic.

Did Keith have a daughter they knew nothing about? Had he been married before? What was Jess getting herself into? A tangled web. He hoped not.

"Who is Vicki?"

"She's my sister. Sorry. Of course, you haven't met Vicki yet. She says I'm crazy if I let Jessica get away."

A comfortable peace settled over them. Relieved, Seth carried his children off to bed, leaving them in their clothes. They were exhausted after the events of the day and he didn't want to disturb their sleep. He knew how they felt. He was tired, too.

Millie had her prayer journal open on the table with a pen poised to make the final entry. She planned to give it to Seth. Prayer points and scriptures from throughout his lifetime were noted in the little black book. After reading several of the recordings, Millie's heart knew this was what she needed to do. Her son would know he was never far away from her or Harold's thoughts. It might be healing for Seth to know that her prayers had surrounded him his whole life.

"We're going to St Oswald's for church this morning and then into Mt Barker to Millie's for lunch."

Seth announced the plans for the day.

"Are we taking a puppy for Courtney?"

Alicia had asked the same question every weekend.

"Not yet, but she'll be ready soon."

Seth had debated with himself several times as to whether or not to tell Alicia and Ryan about Millie being their grandmother. He'd decided it was time. Millie was ecstatic.

'Knock, knock."

Alicia called out as she rapped on Millie's door.

"Who's there?"

Millie responded appropriately.

"Doctor."

Alicia giggled.

"Doctor Who?"

"I'm not Doctor Who!"

"Who are you then?"

They walked in the door and hugged Millie.

"Ryan and Leesh, you are …," Seth paused. "You are Millie's grandchildren."

Ryan scrunched up his face in confusion.

"What do you mean, Dad? Like Auntie Beryl and Uncle Bob – not a real one?"

Seth drew the children to him. *How do I explain this to them? It's hard to try and put it into simple words.*

"Well, now let's take it one step at a time. First of all, I was adopted by Granny and Grandad when I was a baby. Do you understand what that means?"

"I think so. It means they weren't your real Mum and Dad but they wanted a baby and got one from someone else. And it was you."

"That's exactly right, Ryan. And they took care of me and loved me like I love and take care of you."

Millie watched Seth with his children. Her emotions on the brink of spilling over.

"Are we adopted, Dad?"

"No, Leesh. You are both my children. So, now you need to know that Millie was my birth-mother. She and her husband had a baby, that was me, but they couldn't keep me and had to give me away."

"Oh, why did they do that? They should have kept you."

Alicia was confused now. Millie joined the conversation.

"We couldn't, sweetheart, we wanted to but we weren't allowed. It's a bit complicated."

"Maybe we can explain it more when you get a bit older."

"Oh, so it's one of those things. I see. What do we call you, then?"

Alicia never had trouble accepting that some things needed to wait to be understood but Ryan was a bit unsure about that idea.

"I would love you to call me Gran if you think that would be all right."

"Yep. Thanks, Gran. That sounds nice, doesn't it?"

Millie's heart melted. The joy it sent through her was beyond anything she could have imagined.

"It sounds wonderful. Shall we have some lunch?"

Millie reached across and patted Ryan's hand.

"Call me Gran when you're ready, Ryan. No hurry," Millie whispered.

He smiled at his new-found grandmother, thinking it was a lot easier than knowing what to call his mother.

After lunch, the children sat on the couch with 'Gran' and read stories while their father held the prayer journal in his hands. He couldn't believe that Millie had been doing this for his whole life. There was no way he'd be able to read it here. It would have to be done in private because he couldn't be sure how he would react to the words on the page. Millie did show him the last entry, the one where she thanked God for the guidance He'd given to Seth and for providing him with a wonderful family. And praising God for bringing them together again.

The day finally came when the puppy was going to her new home. Courtney and Liam had been to the farm several times to get to know 'Tilly' as they had decided to name her. Ryan had taught her to sit and stay and she was used to being tied up. Tilly had learned her toilet training habits from Mallee and was well socialised with both humans and other dogs.

"Now we take on the job of keeping her busy and training her. I think you might have to give us city kids some tips as we go along. We don't want a naughty, bored dog at our house."

Liam had thought a dog that slept a lot, and that didn't need much entertainment or exercise would be a lot less challenging. Courtney had fallen in love with the red cloud Kelpie puppy when they first saw her. He didn't mind admitting he had, too.

"This is her kennel and lead. Take them with you because she's used to them and they have her smell on them. She hasn't been sleeping with her Mum for a week, so that shouldn't be a problem."

They had used a hot water bottle and a ticking clock to wean her away from Mallee's side. Seth felt comfortable that Tilly was ready to go to her new home but was a bit sad to see her go. Alicia cried.

"What's with the tears?"

Seth rubbed his daughter's back.

"You've wanted Courtney to have her dog for ages."

"I know," Alicia sniffed, "but I didn't think about her not being at our place anymore."

"It's okay. You'll see Tilly at their house sometimes. She'll be excited to see you when you go to visit."

"Will she remember me?"

"I'm sure she will. She's a very smart dog."

That relieved the little girl's sadness and she went off to see their puppy, Bella, in the backyard.

CHAPTER 22

A late phone call, again. Seth expected it could be Felicity. He was right.

"We need to talk," she sounded brusque.

She was back to being the woman in charge. Seth braced himself for what was to come. It had been more than two weeks since the Perth visit and he hadn't heard from her until now. *Help me not to get angry again, Lord. Please.*

"Okay. I'm listening."

He put the ball back in her court. *I'm willing to let you lead this conversation.*

"I don't think the visit worked very well, Seth."

"Felicity, you will have to explain what you mean. I wasn't there."

A soft noise of breath being expelled from her nose could be heard on the line.

"No. Of course not. Alicia was friendly, but she asked a lot of rude questions. You need to teach her what is polite and what isn't."

"She is just a little girl, Felicity."

"Well, Ryan hardly spoke. He was polite enough saying 'yes, please' or 'no, thank you' but we couldn't raise a conversation with him. Not once."

"I'm sorry, Felicity, but you will have to give him time. This is not easy for him."

"Not easy for him! It's not easy for any of us. He didn't eat anything and wouldn't sit next to us either. At least Alicia ate one canape and two petits four. All Ryan did was have an orange juice and take photo after photo. He showed no interest in us whatsoever."

"Don't forget he's only eight-years-old and his photographs are good, Felicity. He has some great shots of the wildflowers. And a photo of you with Oliver and Alicia. You were on the picnic rug in front of the pond with the Pioneer Women's statue and water fountains."

A quiet pause.

"Oh, I didn't know."

"You weren't looking. Oliver was giving you a flute of champagne."

What were you thinking of serving a champagne brunch with kids? That's why Ryan didn't want anything to eat. It was all too fancy for him.

Seth had to wonder if the water spurting out of the top of Oliver's head in the picture was deliberate. The fountain spray wouldn't have been noticeable if Ryan had moved a little to the right, or the left, for that matter. Alicia had laughed when she saw the photo proclaiming Oliver looked like a whale. It had taken a great deal of effort not to laugh with her.

"We can send you a copy of the photo if you like?"

"No, thanks. That won't be necessary."

"What is it you want to say, Felicity? If the short visit isn't working, I can't see how a few days or a week would make it any better."

"No. No, that's not what I want."

Another quiet pause, then …

"Bloody Oliver, it's all his idea," she whispered under her breath.

The comment concerned Seth.

"Are you planning on seeing the children again? At all?"

"That's just the thing. I think it might be better to wait until they are a bit older."

"Why would it be better?"

"Seth, stop being picky. You know they'd be able to communicate on a more mature level."

"I'm not picky, Felicity. You can't expect a friendship with them when they grow up if they don't see you now while they're young. Either you want a relationship with your son and daughter, or you don't. You need to make a decision one way or the other."

He remained calm but he wanted to yell at her. *How dare you! You want what you can't have without making a sacrifice. Isn't that what parents are supposed to do? Well, some do. But you, Felicity, are not one of them.*

"This conversation isn't helpful, Seth."

No, of course not.

"Maybe you need a bit more time to think about it, Felicity. I have to tell you that if you can't commit to regular short visits, then I'll submit your letter to be used in a court action. I expect it would help determine a ruling which would favour me as the children's sole custodian."

"There's no need to get nasty, Seth."

"It's not nasty. I'm telling you the truth."

"All right then, let me think about it. I'll get back to you on it."

"When can I expect a call?"

"Oh, Seth, you are impossible. I don't know. You will have to wait until I work it out."

"Okay, but if I don't hear from you before Christmas, be assured, I will take this to court."

Felicity gave a frustrated sigh and said a polite goodbye.

Well, that's it then. I've gone and done it now but somehow I think I'll hear from her soon.

Seth didn't have to wait long. A few days later, Felicity rang again with another suggestion.

"If you take the children to Bunbury and they stay with my parents, I can see them there. What do you think about that idea?"

"I'll agree to a trial, Felicity. How much time do you anticipate spending with them?"

"Oh, not too long. Oliver has a beach house at Dunsborough and we can pop up to Bunbury for a quick trip, do some shopping and stop in at Mum and Dad's."

Seth couldn't believe it. *Yeah, and leave all the work to Nanna and Pop Norman but she'll get the cream for the few minutes she's prepared to give of her precious time. Argghh,* he felt like refusing but knew that wouldn't work either.

"Have you spoken to Nanna and Pop about this yet? Your Dad has recovered but it might be too much for them."

"Recovered from what?"

"His heart attack. Oh, Felicity, don't tell me you didn't know. That was nearly a year ago."

"They never told me." She sounded cross. "How come you know about it?"

"We stay in touch, Felicity. I ring every second Sunday and they talk to the kids. Ryan and Alicia were there for Christmas. It was a late harvest and I couldn't stop work in December. Nanna and Pop wanted them to go for a few days but I wouldn't let them stay for their swimming lessons in January."

"Huh, I never knew about any of that."

"Could be because you don't contact them very often."

"Oh, here you go again. Picking on me."

The truth hurts or if the cap fits … several other sayings came to Seth's mind.

"You didn't say whether or not you've spoken to them."

"I'm sure Mum and Dad will be okay about it. They've been at me for not going to see them lately. Now I know why. They should have told me. This plan would have a twofold benefit then, wouldn't it?"

"I suppose so."

Seth thought the benefit would apply to the kids getting to spend time with their grandparents. Nanna and Pop would love to see them. Maybe it could work.

"Well?"

"All right, we can give it a try. Let me know soon because I'll have hay to cut in a few weeks and then I'll be helping with the grain harvest in Tambellup. You know I trade my time for using equipment with the Petersen's. The trip will have to be arranged around my farm responsibilities."

"Always the farm ..."

She left the words hanging there.

"It's my job, Felicity. It's what I do."

"Yes, yes. I know."

The response was delivered with an exasperated tone.

"Felicity, do you plan to commit to these visits for a few times?"

Seth wanted to know how much effort she would put in.

"Maybe over the summer but probably not too often in the winter months."

So it's conditional, as well, to suit the lifestyle.

"Mmm, I admit that could make things difficult." *Stop this, Seth, it's not healthy*, he chastised himself.

"Yes. So we are agreed?"

"Yes, Felicity."

"Good. Best you prepare the children for the occasion a bit better this time."

That nearly did it. Seth bit his tongue.

"I shall try."

"Okay, goodbye then."

"Goodbye, Felicity."

He hung up, trying not to slam the receiver into its cradle.

What did I ever see in that woman?

"Lord, I'm sorry. Forgive me for letting Felicity rile me up again. I can't see any of this working well. Help me to do the right thing for Alicia and Ryan."

His plea for help went out to the Lord, who hears and answers prayer. All he had to do now was wait.

CHAPTER 23

School finished on Thursday 10th December and it was Alicia's birthday. Ryan's birthday had been two days earlier. On Wednesday night, the evening between both birthdays they'd had a special dinner at home with Millie, Courtney and Liam. Tilly, the puppy, had come with them. Courtney provided a lasagne at the kids' request. Seth put together a tossed salad and garlic bread, and Millie made a big chocolate cake decorated with Smarties for dessert. Nine blue candles for Ryan were placed on one side with seven yellow ones for Alicia on the other. The children were delighted with their gifts and sharing a special time with their new-found Gran.

Friday was set as the travel day to Bunbury for the pre-arranged visit with Felicity at her parents' house. Seth asked Jessica and Keith if they could take Alicia and Ryan over there. He was going to Tambellup on Friday and Jess wasn't rostered on that weekend. They had been planning to visit his sister, Vicki, who lived in nearby Capel. The kids would return with Keith to stay at Annie and Tom's while Seth was away.

"Right, kids, are you ready to go?"

Jess checked to make sure they had everything they needed. Keith packed the car with luggage and pillows and books and toys. He had no idea children needed this much stuff.

"Here is something for you from us, too."

Jessica gave them matching wrapped presents.

"Happy birthday."

"Ooh, thank you so much." Alicia was effusive in her response. "Wow, I love it."

"Thanks, Auntie Jess." Ryan was much more subdued. He still wasn't sure about this idea of having to see his Mum again, but he couldn't wait to see Nanna and Pop.

Jessica gave them a sticker book and a kaleidoscope in the hope that it would keep them occupied on the three-and-a-half-hour drive. The gifts were a hit and kept them busy for quite some time. They had morning tea along the way and a toilet-stop before setting off again.

"The ants go marching one-by-one, hurrah, hurrah ..." they all sang the song. Jess added, "the little one stopped to scratch his bum, and they all go marching down to the ground to get out of the rain. Boom, boom," the kids laughed so hard they had tears running down their faces. Keith was undone as well.

"Where did you learn that?" he wanted to know.

"Not telling," she replied.

"I can see that seems to be a habit of yours."

They laughed together and listened to the children talk as they swapped their kaleidoscopes.

"Look at this one, Leesh. Be careful not to move it, or it'll shift again."

"Aw, that's pretty..."

Keith looked across at Jess and smiled. He'd never known the joy that children could be until the O'Reilly family had moved to the vineyard. He found Jimmy and Jon an interesting pair and Bronte was a little sweetheart. Now he could see the special love shared between an auntie and her nephew and niece.

Vicki was married for six months before her husband had a horse-riding accident and died. She mourned Daniel's loss for years and wasn't interested in dating again. Maybe they had more in common than he'd realised. *Look at what I've missed out on,* he thought. *Jess is the best thing that's ever happened to me.*

"Okay kids, you'll have to tell us which house is Nanna and Pop's."

Jessica had the address but wanted the kids to have the anticipation of arriving by giving directions.

"It's pink and blue, Auntie Jess," Alicia announced.

"She means the bricks are sort of pink and the roof is blue." Ryan corrected Alicia's description. "And there's a book leaf pine near the letterbox. That's what Pop said it was called. It's kind of flat but shaped like a cone at the same time."

"That sounds very interesting, Ry." His auntie beamed a genuine smile at him. "Keep looking and let us know when it gets close."

"There it is," they both called out.

They were right. The house had plain salmon-coloured bricks and blue roof tiles. Nanna and Pop were watching for them and ran outside as soon as they arrived.

"You're here, at last."

Their grandparents greeted them with hugs and kisses and exclamations about how much they'd grown. Lunch was on the table with more birthday presents for Alicia and Ryan. Nanna hadn't posted them since she knew they were coming to visit. Jessica introduced Keith and they were invited to stay for lunch. Seth had warned them to expect Nanna and Pop Norman's generous hospitality and they accepted the kind offer.

The rosewood dining table was set for six. They pulled out burgundy and gold regency striped upholstered chairs and sat down. Drinks were poured into crystal glasses by Pop and they began to eat their meal.

"Jessica, we're so pleased to see you, it's been far too long. We're glad you've come today. And Keith, tell us about yourself."

Nanna and Pop, as they liked to be called, were comfortable people to be around. Jessica had never understood how their daughter ended up being so frosty in comparison to their warm personalities. They sat around the table drinking coffee. The children played with their new gifts on the floor.

"It's a long story," Keith chuckled.

"We're not going anywhere. Have you got time to tell it?" Pop asked.

Keith looked across to Jess, who shrugged and shook her head. It was okay with her. They couldn't see Vicki until she finished at around five o'clock when she shut her Vet surgery. It didn't take long to drive from Bunbury to Capel and they weren't in a hurry.

"I grew up in Perth, went to a public school and then on to university. You know, all that kind of stuff but I think my life changed when I decided to go north."

"North? As in the north-west of our state?" Nanna wanted to know.

"Yes, the Pilbara. Tom Price, Paraburdoo, Dampier, that area."

"Oh, so you worked at the iron-ore mines?"

"I suppose you could say that."

Keith was a little bit evasive, which piqued Jessica's interest. She hadn't heard much about this part of his life yet.

"What, exactly, does that mean? Tell us more, Keith. Please," she begged.

"I worked for Hancock Mining as a surveyor and geologist in 1965. There was a lot more ore out there than anyone realised."

"It hadn't hit it's boom time at that stage though, had it?" Pop asked.

"No, that came a bit later on."

"Did you like living in the heat, humidity and with all the flies?"

"Not particularly, but you get used to it. I was busy and didn't have anyone to worry about but myself. I had an air-conditioned car and donga. That gave me some relief to the over 40° temperatures in the summer. Being able to sleep in the air-con made a big difference."

"Excuse my ignorance, but what is a 'donga'?"

Nanna felt a bit embarrassed. Keith smiled. Mining terms were a thing of the past but were still ingrained in him.

"A donga is a transportable single person's room. It fits onto the back of a truck and can be shifted around easily. It was the best way to accommodate workers in the mines at that stage. Everyone had their own space with a bed, wardrobe, desk and chair. Nothing flash and we had portable toilet blocks. Later on, the big companies developed housing estates or multi-storey quarters with dining rooms and recreation facilities."

"Oh, I see."

"But before any of that developed we used to sleep in a swag. In the winter, the days were beautiful and warm but it would be freezing during the night. Most people don't know that."

"Huh, no. I've never thought about it before. What sticks in your memory most about the place?"

"Sticks is the right word. The red soil gets into every nook and cranny and never goes away. And always feeling damp, or wet, and having to drink plenty of water. The cost of food was astronomical and getting fresh fruit and vegetables was rare. Facing cyclonic winds and torrents of rain was pretty frightening, too. I guess they're some of the things you don't ever forget."

"It's an interesting life you've had, Keith. How long were you up there?"

"About ten years."

"That long?" Jessica was surprised. "Did you work for Hancock Mining all that time?"

"No, I ventured out on my own after two years and lodged a mining lease for mineral exploration. It took nearly three years to work through all the processes and I was rapt when I discovered high-grade ore on my claim."

"Wow, you had your own iron-ore company?"

"Yes," he smiled. "Pilbardi Iron was my business. I arranged for the ore to be transported from my pit to Paraburdoo, and Hamersley Iron railway line took it through to the port at Dampier."

"So that would've been when the profits and shares skyrocketed, wasn't it?"

Pop had been calculating the time frame to the early 1970's by then.

"Yes."

"Did you make much money?"

"Yes."

"Really?" Jess's eyes widened.

"Yep, a small fortune." Keith grinned and had a bit of a laugh. "I sold it off to one of the big mining companies two years ago. I'd already made a lot of money from it, but the sale secured a huge sum. They're the winners, though, because the mine has been expanded and still has huge potential to be tapped into."

"You should've hung onto it, son." Pop shook his head.

"No, I'd had enough by then. It was all paperwork after the thrill of discovery and development. It was timely and I'm not sorry."

The children had climbed onto their grandparent's knees and listened to the conversation.

"Are you rich? Like a millionaire?"

"Alicia," Nanna reprimanded, "You don't ask people questions like that."

"It's all right, I'm not offended." Keith bent down and whispered in Alicia's ear, "Yes, I am but it's our secret. Okay?"

The little girl clapped her hands and put her finger over her mouth to say 'shhh' with a twinkle in her eye.

"Jess. I think it's time to get a move on, hey?"

"Okay. Thanks, Nanna and Pop. Especially for asking Keith all those questions, I know more about him now than I did before."

"You're welcome," Nanna smiled. "So, you'll pick the children up on Sunday afternoon?"

"Yes, at about two o'clock. Is that okay?"

"Sure is. We are going to have a wonderful time together. See you then."

Ryan knew he'd have a nice time with Nanna and Pop, but he still felt uneasy about the inevitable visit with his mother.

CHAPTER 24

Keith looked across at Jessica while she put her seat belt on. He couldn't explain, even to himself, how much he loved this woman. She was subtly attractive to look at and had an extraordinary personality. Jess was warm and kind and … he couldn't think of the right words, but he knew she was a treasure beyond compare to anything he'd had in his life before.

"Jess, there's a few things I wanted to say back there but not with others around."

"Oh, what was that?" she looked puzzled.

"Mostly that when I was up north, well, I learned a lot about myself."

"Like what?"

"That I couldn't control everything in my life. I would lay awake in my swag and look up at an endless black sky with a multitude of stars I'd never noticed before. I realised there had to be a creator and I had a responsibility to be answerable to Him."

"Wow, that's pretty profound."

"It was, but you know how life goes. You get busy and slack and there wasn't anyone for me to talk to about it all. I guess you'd say I lost some of that awe for a while. What I want to tell you is how much living down here has slowly changed my perspective."

"What do you mean?"

"Being among Christian people re-ignited my sense of unworthiness. They are all shining lights and my flicker had just about gone out."

"That happens sometimes."

"I saw people change because of God working in their lives. It hit home, hard. I ended up having to deal with my sinfulness. Fortunately, God's mercy extends to people like me, too."

Jessica smiled and put her hand out to hold his. She had tears in her eyes. Up until this point, she hadn't been sure where Keith stood in his faith. But here he was bearing his soul, and it endeared him to her even more. She had been drawn to him when they had met, the silver streaks at his temples and crow's feet at the corners of his eyes enhanced his handsome face. She felt a sense of purpose in his confession.

They pulled into the driveway at Vicki's house and Keith pulled out his key to the front door. There was a note on the table for him.

'Welcome. Make yourselves at home. Keith, you can have my room and I'll share with Jessica in the spare room with the twin beds.' Keith chuckled after he finished reading it aloud.

"I think she's making sure we don't get up to any hanky panky. My sister is such a prude. I'll have to reassure her that it was never going to be a problem."

Jess smiled at him, knowing he had the same values as her. She trusted him completely.

"Now, I want to show you Vicki's rose garden out the back. It's stunning and you are going to love it. Come on."

He held out his hand, took hers and led her outside. He was right. An array of hybrid tea, David Austin and floribunda roses abounded in beds, on trellises and in massive pots. The couple wandered through the garden reading name labels and enjoying the heady perfumes. Keith sat Jess on a seat under an arbour adorned with masses of pink and cream full-cupped Pierre de Ronsard blooms, their gentle aroma filling the arched hollow. It was magical. Keith got down on one knee.

"Jessica Tatiana Jarvis, will you marry me?"

He held out a small dark blue box and opened it. A stunning brilliant-cut diamond surrounded by sapphires peeked out of its white velvet nest.

After Jess recovered from the shock, with eyes shining, she responded.

"Keith. Yes, I will."

"Phew, that's a relief."

She giggled with joy.

"What an amazing day."

He put the ring on her finger, jumped up, dragged Jess to her feet and wrapped her in his arms. She looked deep into his eyes and all she could see was unabashed love for her. She tipped her head up and they kissed. A deep, tender, longing kiss that took their breath away. Keith spoke in an emotion-charged voice.

"I love you so much, Jessica. I never want to be without you."

"And I love you, Keith Crawford. You mean everything to me."

They remained wrapped in a warm embrace, smiling, kissing and laughing together until Vicki happened upon them. The couple looked at each other and chuckled.

"What's going on?"

Jessica's response to Vicki's question was to hold out her hand with the engagement ring flashing in the late afternoon sunlight.

"Awesome. I get to have a sister, at last. And I have to say, I've never known my big brother to be more content in his whole life. That's because of you, Jessica. Congratulations."

"Can I go and ring Seth, and let him know?" Jess turned to Keith.

"He'll be out in the paddock. Besides, he already knows."

Keith's smirk left Jessica open-mouthed.

"He does?"

"Yep, I spoke to him last week. I didn't do the 'asking for your hand in marriage' thing, but I let him know I planned to propose. He said he wasn't surprised after seeing us together and thought it would come sooner or later. He's happy it's sooner."

"When will you get married?"

Vicki couldn't dampen her excitement.

"As soon as possible." Keith chuckled saying this with a twinkle in his eye. He placed his arm around Jessica. "That's if it's all right with you."

"Of course, it is."

The smile on her face widened.

"You need to be aware, Mr Crawford, that it will have to be the proverbial white wedding with all the trimmings."

"Why is that?"

Jessica's eyes softened and a watery sheen glazed over them.

"Because it's what my Mum would've wanted for me."

A quiet pause sat in the sentimental moment.

"That's lovely, Jessica. She'd be very proud of you." Vicki stepped forward and hugged her future sister-in-law.

Keith had a lump in his throat that wouldn't be swallowed. His love for this young woman seeped through him. *And I'm the lucky man,* this thought seemed somewhat sappy but it was no less significant in his mind.

Saturday afternoon came around far too quickly. Nanna and Pop were as nervous as the children while they waited for the arrival of Felicity. They hadn't met Oliver before and it had been over eighteen months since they had any contact with their daughter. And that phone call was when she needed to borrow some money for the expensive bond on the new rental apartment she'd acquired. Admittedly, Felicity had repaid it within six months. They'd despaired over their poor relationship and hoped this could be a new beginning for all of them.

"I think they're here, Nanna." Alicia had kept watch at the window. "I'm sure that's Oliver's car."

The doorbell chimed. Pop had volunteered to bear the responsibility of answering the door on their arrival.

"Hello, Felicity."

He reached out to his daughter with open arms and received a formal half-hearted hug. The same was offered to her mother. The children stood back and watched. Felicity turned to Oliver to introduce him to her parents.

"Mum, Dad, this is Oliver."

She beamed a happy smile at him. Oliver stretched out his hand to Pop.

"Hello, Dad. Nice to meet you."

He slapped the older man on the back and stepped across to embrace Felicity's mother.

"And, Mum. How are you?"

Her parents were a little confronted by his familiarity. They struggled to make conversation after the encounter and noticed a huge solitaire diamond and shining gold wedding band on Felicity's left hand. It wasn't long before the children were taken off to the local milk bar. Ice-cream was the only positive notion they took away from their previous visit, hence the decision to allow them a choice from the freezer in the cafe. Alicia picked a Drumstick and Ryan had a Giant Sandwich.

"How are you enjoying your holidays, children?" Felicity asked as they sat at the table by the window while waiting for their drinks to be served.

"We only finished on Thursday," Ryan responded politely. He'd been drilled before they left home by his father to make sure he answered their questions. "But we've got a new puppy and I've been looking after Bella."

"Oh, yes, of course. I forgot state schools finish up about a week to ten days after private schools." She addressed Oliver with her comment. Ryan looked away so she wouldn't see his hurt feelings. It didn't matter to him that they had to stay at school longer. It was just what they did.

"Did you give the dog her name?" Oliver asked Ryan.

"We chose a good name for her together. She's called Bella after the Cranbrook Bell[8]. It's a wildflower that grows near our farm."

"Yes, that would make sense," Felicity added. "Seth is into native plants and wildflowers in the district. Takes a million photographs every season." She rolled her eyes. Oliver nodded in understanding. The coffee cups were placed in front of the adults and glasses of orange juice were given to the children.

"Alicia, you're quiet today."

The little girl wanted to say, *'You forgot about our birthdays.'*

She looked across the table at her brother. Ryan's eyes filled with a tender warning.

"I have to be careful not to say wrong things," she looked up at her mother and replied politely.

"Oh, so your father did talk to you about that. Good." Felicity passed a serviette to Alicia. "Here, you need to wipe your chin. You have ice-cream dripping everywhere."

---

8 Cranbrook Bell

Within an hour the children were dropped off back at their grandparents. Their early return surprised Nanna and Pop, and they felt obliged to offer a cup of tea.

"Oh, no. We've just had a coffee. We're heading back to Dunsborough now. Thanks for everything." Felicity, satisfied with the excursion, turned and bounced back to the car. Now she and Oliver could return to their holiday by the beach.

"Don't say a word, love."

Pop looked at his wife with a nod of his head toward their grandchildren. Nanna knew Pop was reading her mind. His thoughts weren't far from hers. They were disappointed, but went and put the kettle on to enjoy a cup of tea and play Go Fish with Alicia and Ryan. They cherished the time with them. They saw a great deal of their other grand-kids who all lived nearby and visited regularly.

Seth rang later that evening. Pop answered the phone and had a quick chat before Nanna spoke to him and explained the visit in detail. She said Ryan seemed a lot happier when he returned and Alicia was withdrawn initially but didn't take long to resume her usual bouncy countenance. They agreed that this approach would be the best option for the future.

CHAPTER 25

Seth picked up Millie's prayer journal and opened it to the bookmark where he'd left it at his last reading. He hadn't come back to it for a few weeks because it played havoc with his emotions. Never would he have believed his birth-mother's insight into what was happening in his life while he was growing up could be true except that it was right here in black and white. There was no question about it being the work of the Holy Spirit. Things like when he had the measles; and the day he fell off the tractor and broke his arm and had to have surgery. The notes were not specific, but there was a defining prayer that connected to those events. He began to read again.

My dear son, today you will turn 21. I'm sure you are a man that your adoptive parents, and Harold and I, would be proud of. Stand tall, embrace your future and the plans God has for you. Wherever you are and however you celebrate this day, do so with much joy. We would have loved to share this special time with you. God bless you, son.

His twenty-first birthday had been a community affair with a barn dance and dinner at the Hall in Cranbrook. Neighbours, school friends and family, had gathered for the occasion. It was a wonderful evening. He'd been showered with gifts and hugs and slaps on the back. The warmth of the memory radiated through him. And without even knowing about it, in some small way, his biological parents had been a part of it.

The ribbon of the journal marked a page he hadn't read before, and when he opened it, he noticed a splotch stain on the page. He read the prayer.

Lord, I have a heavy heart today. I feel a burden for our son and the need to pray for him. Whatever this is about, I give it to you. You know what he is facing, you are aware of the help that needs to come his way. Provide it, please, Lord. Guide and direct his path. I pray this in the name of Jesus Christ. Amen.

It must have been a teardrop. Millie's earnest prayer had caused her to cry when she wrote the words. He looked at the date and tried to recall what was happening in his life at the time. He closed his eyes and bit his lips as they curled inward. How could he forget. He'd wanted all the pain to stop – even the responsibility of the kids that day didn't seem incentive enough to keep living. He felt unloved, unlovable, alone and miserable with no hope for the future. A foreboding enveloped him as irrational thoughts seemed like his only option. What could he do? That was the question he'd been pondering when a vehicle pulled up outside and then there was a loud knock on the door.

His instinct to answer it couldn't be ignored but he thought he'd get rid of the person and then make his plans. Whatever that would be - which he still hadn't decided.

Seth was dishevelled, unshaven and hadn't showered in days. The kids were with his parents in town to give him some time on his own. It probably hadn't been the best idea. A looming figure stood looking out to the paddock and all Seth could see was the man's profile. The distinct features were notable with a long nose and grey bristled eyebrows standing out on a broad forehead. It wasn't anyone he thought he knew although there was a familiarity about the man that Seth couldn't place. He opened the door.

"Yeah, mate. What can I do for you?"

"Hi there. I think I'm lost and I hope you wouldn't mind giving me some directions."

"Sure. Where do you want to go?"

"I've been asked to pop in and see Fred and Eunice Hampton. They live on this road somewhere but I can't find the right turn off."

"You're close. They're just a few more kilometres along the road that way." He pointed in the direction he needed to go. "It's a bit tricky because the turn off to the property looks like an open paddock with only a track to follow. Fred's been going to do something about signage for ages. Probably never will."

The man's clear blue eyes looked straight into Seth's soul. He shuddered at the exposure.

"Have we met before?"

"Not sure."

"Maybe at St Oswald's."

Ah, that was it. He'd seen the man at the church when he'd been for Christmas and Easter services. He was the minister from Mt Barker, and this was becoming a bit more of an intrusion than he'd hoped. He needed to get rid of him.

"Yes, that's probably it. I hope you find the place."

Seth went to close the door but the man put his hand out.

"I'm Bob Webber. It's nice to meet you."

Seth shook it.

"Yeah, I'm Seth."

He stood there not knowing what to do, or say.

"Are you all right, son? I fear you're in need of a helping hand and I've got a pretty big one right here."

The older man smiled and lifted his palm. It was enough to crack through Seth's fragile emotions. He desperately needed someone to talk to, and if he didn't do it today, there might not be a chance of any more tomorrows. He shrugged his shoulders, doubtful that anyone could say anything that might make a difference.

"Any chance of a cup of tea?" Bob asked. "Or just a drink of water."

He prayed the young fellow would offer him one. He didn't like the thought of leaving him alone in the state he'd found him. Seth was hurting, bad, he could tell.

"Um, well ..."

Seth was embarrassed. The house was a mess and he didn't have any milk or biscuits to offer. Bob read through the pause, suspicious that he wasn't comfortable with asking him in.

"It's a beautiful afternoon. How about we sit out here on the verandah? Would that be okay?" Bob's peaceful demeanour had a calming effect on Seth.

"Yeah, sure. All I've got is black tea."

"That'll be fine, thanks."

While Seth went into the kitchen to make the hot drinks, Bob prayed. Prayer for wisdom, prayer for an opening to talk to Seth about God's love and peace. Prayer for healing of this young man's heart. Seth came back through the screen door with two cups.

"Sorry, I look disgraceful," he'd attempted to tidy himself up a bit.

"How about telling me what's going on? Would I be right in thinking you're not in a good place? I don't want to seem rude but I know when a person needs to share a burden. It comes with the job."

Bob's warmth and smile relaxed Seth. Four hours later, the refreshment Seth experienced from his time discussing his situation with Bob made him feel so much better. And it wasn't from the cup of tea.

"I'll head on up the road to the Hampton's place before the sun sets, Seth. Can I come to see you again?"

"Yeah, I'd appreciate it. Thanks, Bob."

And Millie had prayed for him that very day. Seth tipped his head back and looked at the ceiling of his bedroom and closed his eyes.

"Lord, you heard Millie's prayer and answered it. Didn't you?"

His voice echoed in the silence.

"I know it, Lord. There's no other explanation. It wasn't a mistake at all. You planned it to rescue me."

Seth's wonder at the guarding and guiding hand of God Almighty working in his life to turn it around stunned him.

"You loved me that much, Lord. I felt alone but you were there. You sent someone to help me even though I didn't know it was intentional at the time. How can I ever thank you?"

Peace surrounded him as he remembered his response to that urgent knocking. It had been in his heart, too, not just at his front door. A week later he'd given his life, his future and all that he had to God. He'd dumped his burdens at the foot of Jesus' cross with the sinner's prayer acknowledging his need to be saved, and walked away relieved. Joy and light were his companions at the end of that tunnel. There was no question about it, and he'd wanted to search out God's plan and follow it into a new future.

It reminded him of the burning desire he'd had at that point in his life to please the Lord. His struggle over the difficulty of the divorce and the contention with Felicity had overwhelmed him. Getting stuck up on the hill in the Stirling Ranges was another reminder that he had to trust God in everything. He'd been rescued twice, and Seth found blessings in both situations. Sometimes bad things turned out to be for his good. There had to be a lesson in that to share with someone else one day.

He prayed that God might use him in the same way as he had used Bob. The Reverend had been obedient to God's calling and it made a difference in his life. As it had turned out, Fred and Eunice wanted to talk to Reverend Webber and ask him to speak to Seth. That's how concerned they'd been for him, but God beat them to it.

CHAPTER 26

Bob picked up the triangular name stand on his desk with Reverend Robert J Webber engraved on it. Even though he knew the time was coming to retire, he wasn't ready. He put the nameplate back beside the lamp where it belonged. He'd just finished speaking with the Bishop, perhaps the assistance and mentoring of a young deacon would lighten his load. The phone conversation whirled around in his head.

"Bob, how are you?"

"I'm fine, thanks, Bishop. I have good days and not so good ones but on the whole I'm coping. I haven't shared the news with anyone else because Beryl and I feel it's better that way, for now. Everyone knows I've been treated for asthma for years but the diagnosis of emphysema will come as a surprise to them."

"I've been concerned about you and your health issues. Are you sure you want to continue working? You don't have to, you know."

"I know, and the time will come soon enough but not yet."

"I have news. Perth diocese have a young man who grew up in Albany looking for a country placement in the south-west. I think this would benefit both of you. I'd like him to join you and, God willing, he could be made priest in 12-18 months. You never know, he might even be able to attempt to fill your big shoes."

The Bishop had chuckled at his attempt of humour, knowing Bob had huge feet and wore a size 12 shoe.

"Maybe that's the solution to all of this."

"I think it could work out well for both of you."

"What can you tell me about him?"

"He's a keen and sharp young fellow. And I mean, young. He's only 23 but is committed to life-long service in the Anglican Church. I think the time you could give him would be a blessing to both of you. His name is Joshua Bennett. He's an ordained deacon and ready to spread his wings."

Bob was surprised. Such a young man, but if it was God's leading and because it was the Bishop's suggestion, he needed to give it sincere consideration. The Bishop had chatted about a few other things and offered God's blessings to him and Beryl before he hung up. Bob was left hopeful that the four parishes would be supportive of the proposed appointment.

He expected part of the Bishop's plan for Joshua was for him to receive guidance through his inevitable youthful enthusiasm. Bob remembered some of the mistakes he'd made when he started out in ministry and how some of it could have been avoided if he'd had a mentor. His biggest regret was that his father's ministerial experience hadn't been available to him at the time.

His thoughts turned toward the people he'd come to know and love. After nine years of being a part of this fellowship, he'd grown meaningful relationships with them. Bob wasn't sure how his congregation would react to the news of his illness. They were kind people and even though some were stuck in their ways they were sincere in their faith. His desire was to earnestly pray for them. Bob read some scripture, then opened his heart before God.

"Lord, I give you the praise and glory you deserve. I come humbly before you seeking your direction, especially about the Bishop's request. This young fellow coming here may well be part of your will for him and for me. Give me the guidance I need, Lord, to trust you for what's best for your people: these people of your heart, the flock you have allowed me to shepherd, and I bring them before you today."

Bob paused and waited on the Holy Spirit's guidance before he continued.

"Meet their needs, I pray, in each of their situations. Put your hand of mercy upon those who are weak, heal those who are unwell and encourage those who need uplifting. I thank you for their lives and what they have given back to me, and for their love and support. Thank you for those times when it felt like some might never understand your truths. Those were the days when I had to wait on you even more for your divine revelation. May your flock continue to grow in their faith every day."

He rested his elbows on the desk and placed his head in his hands, meditating quietly. Beryl paused at the door, fully aware of the Holy Spirit at work. She walked away with the cup of tea, knowing she could make a fresh one when her husband was done praying. It might be a while.

"I commit our brother, Seth, into your loving hands, Father. Bless him through the struggles he's been faced with recently. Thank you for drawing him to yourself. Give him the wisdom he needs for the decisions he has to make. Protect Alicia and Ryan, Lord, and help them to cope with the recent changes in their lives. Bless Millie. Lord,

I believe your hand has gone before them. Thank you for reuniting mother and son in such extraordinary circumstances. You have shown Seth clearly that Millie is indeed his birth-mother. Praise your name."

Bob's heart filled with thanksgiving and he savoured the moment.

"And for Jessica and Keith, Lord, as they plan to marry – may they commit their lives to each other before you and in you. Lead them and guide them, bless them, Lord. I ask for wisdom for Annie and Tom as they raise the O'Reilly children and their granddaughter. Father, wherever Freya may be, please be beside her. Call her and bring her back into the fold. May she restore her relationship with her family, and especially little Kaimarie."

The Reverend uttered a single addition to this prayer.

"Please."

His thoughts were prompted to continue in prayer for this group of friends.

"And Courtney and Liam. Lord, it's such a blessing to see them growing closer together and to you. Thank you for providing work at the school for Liam and helping them settle into their new lifestyle here in the country. Bless their friendship with Todd and guide him in his future. Keep them in your care and bless them all abundantly, I pray in Jesus name. Amen."

Beryl walked past and noticed her husband sitting and staring out of the window.

"Hello dear, are you ready for a cup of tea now?"

"Yes, please." His response was enthusiastic.

"You seem a little wistful, dear," Beryl's concern echoed through her words.

"Just a request from the Bishop to consider."

"Oh, and what was that? Am I allowed to know about it?"

Bob explained the gist of the phone call and she had a sense of peace about the idea. She was very aware that her husband wasn't ready to face retirement, and it concerned her.

"I'll keep praying that God will reveal His will. I have a feeling it could be the right thing at the right time."

Beryl smiled at him as she placed two cups on the table and passed Bob the biscuits. He took two.

"Did you know Seth found paperwork attached to his birth certificate that shouldn't have been there. Adoption notices like that are always kept by the Department, not given to adoptive parents. Somebody didn't do their job properly."

"How does that affect Seth?"

"Well, it means he has details of his birth-mother's name that he shouldn't be privy to. But you know what? It leaves no doubt that Millie is his mother. It's her maiden name and signature on that document."

"I heard he looks just like her Harold."

"Yes, I believe so. It's a pity we never got to meet him. He died the year before we came here."

"I'm thrilled for Millie. She's so happy and relieved in many ways. It's exciting when you see these things happen. Don't you think?"

Beryl glanced at Bob, who was looking out the window again. He hadn't heard her.

Oh, well, he's contemplating the future and what its going to bring.

She let it go and cleared the table.

CHAPTER 27

Joshua Bennett whirled around in a circle and pumped his fists in the air. He nearly lost his balance and fell over but managed to grab the back of a chair to steady himself. *Thank you, Lord.* A placement at All Saints Anglican Church in Mt Barker would be his first assignment. The Bishop had confirmed the opportunity to work with Reverend Bob Webber and Joshua was thrilled.

It was only half-an-hour away from home and he'd be able to see more of his family who lived in Albany. Even though things were a bit strained, he had committed to showing them God's loving grace and prayed for them every day. Being the youngest of five, his older siblings considered him spoiled and allowed to get away with many things they hadn't. It had driven a wedge between him and them, although, he and his next closest sister had a good friendship.

Joshua rang his Scripture Union camp director to share the news with someone whom he knew would share in his excitement.

"Steve. I had to ring and let you know I've got a posting in Mt Barker."

"Josh, I'm happy for you. That's wonderful news. God's plans for you are beginning to unfold. When do you start?"

"Next week."

"That soon. Wow. Have you told your family yet?"

"No, but I plan to after this phone call to you."

"How do you think they'll feel about it."

"They are going to have to come to terms with it at some point and accept that I'm going to be a priest."

"Mmm. Tread carefully, Josh."

"I'll be tactful." He took the advice to heart. "I can't wait to meet the people at All Saints and get involved in the church."

Steve smiled. His memories of this young man gave him cause to have a bit of a chuckle. He'd come such a long way and truly had a calling from God. It had been a privilege to be a part of his journey.

It was the first week of January eight years previous when Joshua Bennett turned up at Glen Echo Scripture Union camp at the Kalgan River. The fifteen-year-old boy lived in Albany and arrived at camp early because he didn't have to catch the bus from Perth. His father had dropped him off and left the skinny fair-haired lad standing there with his rucksack unsure of what he should do. The other campers were travelling together down the highway on a bus. They were expected to arrive in about an hour, a bit later than originally planned. Fortunately, Steve had heard the vehicle drive up the track and went to meet him.

"Hello. I'm Steve. Welcome to Glen Echo Farm."

"Hi. I'm Josh."

He appeared a little awkward and his clear blue eyes darted around the campsite. Steve ventured to help him relax.

"So, how did you find out about our camp here?"

"There was a SU holiday camp form on the pin-up board in the school hall. I picked it up and thought I'd like to come. My Dad wasn't too thrilled about spending the money but he's happy to get rid of me for a week. Mum was okay about it."

"Wow. Well, we're glad to have you. Come on, wanna give me a hand here?"

"Yeah, sure."

Josh had picked up his gear and followed him. He managed to tangle ropes, trip over the power cords and spill the cordial on the table in the dining tent. Steve couldn't get annoyed because Josh was a great guy and interesting to talk to. He got on well with the other campers and pitched in, even though he was more often a hindrance than a help.

Kayaking safety drills were the first things they did down at the river. Each camper had to master rolling over and resurfacing in their kayak in case they capsized. Josh had no trouble tipping over and learning how to do the Eskimo Roll. He was stung by bluebottle jellyfish in the river and had to be doused in vinegar. It helped to counteract the pain caused by the stingers that clung to the bare skin on his arms and legs.

Paddling up the river was great fun. Reflections of clouds on the still water were stunning until their group of teenagers paddled through and stirred it up. Josh had loved the night paddle and seeing the bioluminescence glowing in the water. It was something that occurs when a micro-organism in the river water is disturbed by oxygen. The stars on a clear night looked amazing. The challenge of climbing Bluff Knoll at the crack of dawn and then seeing the 360° view blew him away. He had no idea how majestic the whole place was until they'd scaled the heights.

Camp food, the tenting lifestyle and fun activities were new experiences for Josh but he'd loved it all. Joshua had never been to church and had only attended Scripture classes at school. He had a ravenous appetite for understanding what the Bible had to say and belted out the songs with his great singing voice.

Steve was thrilled with the deep conversations they'd shared throughout the week and answering all of Joshua's questions. At the end of the camp, Josh had given his heart to the Lord. They arranged to pick him up for church and drop him off afterwards even though his father was reluctant to let him go. Prayers of the people in the fellowship had encouraged Joshua in his young faith. They stayed in touch after he moved to Perth to study theology. College was where he experienced God's call to ministry within the Anglican Church.

Joshua braced himself for the next phone call he needed to make. His mum answered, which was a relief.

"Hi, Mum. It's me, Josh."

He told her who he was because he and his eldest brother sounded similar when they spoke on the phone. Although, his conversation would be somewhat different given their lifestyles were altogether opposite to each other.

"Hello, son. How are you?"

"Yeah, really good, Mum. I've got some news to share."

The excitement in his voice couldn't be hidden.

"Do tell," she said.

"I've got a job. I'm going to be working at All Saints Church in Mt Barker. Close to home, Mum. I'll be able to visit more often. I can't wait."

"That's nice, Joshua." A halting in the conversation and then ... "I suppose you expect me to tell your father."

"Would you? I'd appreciate it. You know I've been ordained a deacon, Mum, and this job means I'll get the experience I need working with people in the church."

An audible sigh could be heard.

"Okay, but I'll just let him know you've got the job and not all that other stuff. It'll only upset him. You know that, don't you?"

"Yes, Mum, I do. I hope he'll understand. I know this is what I'm meant to do and I have such a peace about it. Thanks, and I love you, Mum."

"I love you, too."

The brief conversation finished and Joshua hung up feeling a little sad that they couldn't share in his joy. He had to pray for them.

"I know it's up to you, Lord, to reach my family's hearts and I pray you'll keep knocking on those doors. Let me be a light to them and help me not to bear resentment toward their attitudes. I want to follow your plan for me and I long for them to come to know you. For their salvation, for their peace and for the plans you have for them, I commit them all to you. In your Holy Name, I pray. Amen."

Josh began to pack his worldly goods into boxes. Mostly books, study notes and several versions of the Bible. He had given notice to the landlord of the furnished apartment he had rented for several years. The Brown's were sorry to see him go. They'd said he'd been a great tenant and they would miss him. He'd miss them too, especially on Wednesday nights when they had dinner together. It was the one night of the week he didn't have to worry about food.

Each Wednesday had become an evening of debate over certain aspects of current affairs. After dinner, a Bible study discussing Scripture and sharing their thoughts was enjoyed around the cleared table. Yes, he would miss these times. But, he knew where he was going was his calling and God's hand would be upon them all wherever they may be.

CHAPTER 28

Celebrations for Kaimarie's first birthday and Keith and Jessica's engagement found the O'Reilly house abuzz with action. Decorations adorned the family room; most of them for Christmas but this room was arrayed with a profusion of pink balloons, candles and flowers. Annie's plans were beginning to take shape. It was December 23, the day before her granddaughter's birthday on Christmas Eve. They were having the celebration earlier because of all the other activities at this time of the year.

Annie made a number 1 shaped cake and decorated it with yellow icing and bright coloured chocolate Smarties. The new Women's Weekly Children's Birthday Cake book displayed various themed cakes with instructions on how to put them together. Jimmy, Jon and Bronte chose the simple cake since Kaimarie was going to be one-year-old. They had fun deciding what they wanted for their birthdays next year. Annie groaned. As if she didn't have enough to do. And the boys wanted a cake each – on the same day: one of the dilemmas of having twins. Twice as much all at once. She smiled at their excitement and wiped the sweat off her forehead with the corner of her apron.

Jessica arranged for Mavis to make an engagement cake and would collect it later in the afternoon. The butter cake and fruitcake covered the catering for dessert. Salads in bowls and barbeque meats in a tray were in the refrigerator. Annie chose to use paper plates and napkins to save time and effort of the washing up afterwards. The other things were set out on the table: knives, forks, sauces, pepper and salt, glasses and plastic cups for the kids. The bread and butter would be put out later. All good to go, she was nearly there, with just a few last-minute things to cook in the oven.

"How about you sit down for a bit, love."

Tom poured a cold Olde Stoney ginger beer for himself and his wife. He sat beside her on one of the chairs outside.

"I hope it cools down a bit soon."

"Yep, me too."

He drank his drink and poured another. Tom had been sweeping the courtyard, setting out tables and chairs and mowing lawns.

"It all looks pretty good."

"Thanks, Tom."

Annie looked at her husband with soft eyes. He returned her look and put an arm around her.

"You do things real nice, Annie. The least I can do is give you a hand when you need it."

Keith and Jess walked around the back of the house and joined them. Jessica had arrived the day before and she'd been helping Annie with food preparations this morning.

"Do you wanna drink, you two?" Tom asked.

"Yes, please." They responded at the same time. Tom went off to get some more glasses and another bottle of ice-cold ginger beer.

"There you go."

"Thanks."

In unison again. They looked at each other and grinned.

"Oh, stop that goin' all mushy and googly-eyed business." Tom joked with them.

"We're heading off to collect the cake soon. We'll be back in about an hour and a half. When do you expect Kate and Jerry to arrive?"

Annie looked at Jess to answer her question.

"They should be here soon."

"Where are you going to put everyone?"

"Kate and Jerry are going into the boys' room 'cos you and Vicki are in Bronte's. And the kids are having a sleepover in the tent ..."

"Which I have to go and put up in a minute," Tom interrupted.

"… with Ryan and Alicia, and Kaimarie is sleeping in the fold-up cot in our room. We've certainly got more than a house full. There's a shuffle going on everywhere."

"What do you mean?" Jess asked.

"Well, Liam and Courtney will be back today from Perth with Liam's parents who arrived from Sydney the day before yesterday. They are going to stay in Millie's house because Joshua Bennett is in the guest room at Courtney's place. And Millie will go out to the farm at Cranbrook with Seth tonight to spend Christmas and New Year with your family."

"Oh, yes. I'd forgotten about that. Too many other things on my mind at the moment."

"Someone around here's been distractin' you, I suspect." Tom's cackle was infectious. They all laughed at him and with him. Jess flashed her engagement ring around in the sunlight to confirm the point before she and Keith set off to get their cake. No sooner had they gone than Kate and Jerry arrived. *Here we go,* Annie thought, *it's all about to happen.*

"Jerry, you're just in time to help me put this big tent up."

Tom had wondered how he was going to manage it by himself.

"Okay. Just let me get unloaded and I'll be right with you."

"You didn't waste any time, Tom. We haven't even darkened your doorstep yet." Kate added, "Where's my girl?"

No sooner had she spoken than Bronte came flying through the glass sliding door to greet her Auntie Kate.

"We're here. And we're staying for Christmas." Kate gathered Bronte in her arms and hugged her.

"Yay." The little girl cheered. They wandered off together, holding hands and chatting away. It had been weeks since they'd seen each other. Jerry stood watching them. Tom noticed.

"That's real special. Don't ya reckon, Jer?"

"Sure is. I can't believe the difference in my wife since we've been coming here."

"Praise the Lord."

"Amen to that," Jerry concluded.

The party was in full swing. Music, talking, kids squawking, people everywhere and unwrapped gifts piled up on the table inside. Annie went to the fridge for some more sausages. The children ate their hot dogs and wanted more than she'd anticipated. The boys' appetites had increased since they were on school holidays. *Using up all that energy,* Annie supposed.

Liam's parents, Vicki Crawford, and Joshua had been introduced to everyone. The friendly atmosphere put the newcomers at ease and the mingling of old and new friends had been successful. Kaimarie, wearing her pretty pink party dress, was passed around happily smiling at everyone and encouraged to say the few words she knew. Mum, Dadda, Bwon, Jim-jim, Jon and doggie was about the extent of her vocabulary. Annie still felt uneasy about their granddaughter calling them Mum and Dad. But, it stood to good reason that she copied the other children in the household.

Kaimarie was getting tired and would need to go to bed soon. Annie got her cake out, put matches and a knife beside it. Time to light the candle and take some photos. She was sad that Freya wasn't here to share the moment. An informal dedication ceremony for Kaimarie was to be held by Joshua. Then Bob was going to offer a blessing over the engaged couple. Everyone crowded into the family room, all eyes on the little girl and the young man.

"Thank you for the warm welcome I've received here tonight. I look forward to the times we will share in the future," Joshua began. "It's an honour, and a pleasure, to bring your attention to a special little girl. Kaimarie will have her first birthday tomorrow." He held her in his arms and tickled her chin, making her jet-black pigtails jiggle when she laughed.

"Such a happy baby and a joy to her grandparents and their children. The love shared in this family is evident. This evening we thank God for the life of Kaimarie and ask that you share in dedicating yourselves to play a part in her life. If you accept this request, please say, We do."

A hearty agreement echoed in the room.

"Let's pray. Lord, we ask that Kaimarie will grow in faith, that she will know the love of God and come to know Jesus as her Saviour and Lord. We thank you for placing her in the care of Annie and Tom, Jonathan, James and Bronte. We thank God for the friends that surround this family who love the Lord and are willing to participate in nurturing this little one and stand alongside them in prayerful and practical support. We pray for Freya and ask God's blessing and protection upon her wherever she may be. Please extend your mercy to her, we ask in Jesus' name, Amen. And may we all enjoy a slice of this cake."

Moist eyes were wiped, and a giggle followed Joshua's cake announcement. An emotional moment, not seen by the other guests, filled the heart of one who kept her distance. The candle was lit and the children volunteered to help Kaimarie blow it out. Annie placed her hand over the child's and together they cut the cake.

The baby was put into bed and she'd fallen straight to sleep. Annie put the urn on to boil while Bob asked Jessica and Keith to come forward.

"Now it's my turn," Bob announced, "to have the pleasure of asking God's blessing on this happy couple." Jessica and Keith turned to face their group of friends. "We share in your joy and pray for your time of preparation for the big day. There may be times in the decision-making and rush to get everything done when you need to stop. Remember to reflect and focus on God and your love for each other; know that it is He who holds your future in His hands, and it is His delight for you to share in the bonds of marriage. May our Holy God of the universe, of our hearts and lives, bless you abundantly today and every day."

Bob prayed for them and then announced there would be more cake to go with a cuppa. A cheer rang out and Jessica handed out wedding invitations. The date was set. They would be married on Saturday 6th February, 1982.

"That's only six weeks away. Are you sure you'll have enough time to get everything ready?" Millie was concerned that they were rushing things.

"We have to be back in time for Keith to prepare for the grape harvest and I'll only have two weeks leave before I have to be back at the hospital."

"Oh, that makes sense. No point in waiting if you know you're meant to be together."

"Especially at our ages," Jessica smiled, knowing it was what people probably thought. Both she and Keith knew it was the right time.

"Vicki will be my bridesmaid, and Keith's asked Jerry to be best man," Jess confided to Annie and Millie. "It'll be a small wedding but Keith has some grand ideas that I have to accept. After all, it's his wedding, too."

"Ooh, I wonder what he's got planned?" Millie's face glowed with anticipation.

"Annie, can we ask Bronte to be a flower girl with Alicia? We'd like the boys to be ushers at the door of the church and Ryan will be a ring-bearer. Do you think they'd be okay with that?"

"I'm sure they will be delighted, Jess."

A light shone in their eyes at the prospect of it all. The women chatted about bride and bridesmaid's dresses and colours. Annie's mind was in a whirl. It was going to be a busy season with Christmas, New Year, swimming lessons and a wedding the weekend after the children returned to school.

Bob and Beryl sat with Liam's parents while they chatted, ate their cake and had a cuppa. He could hear the conversation behind him where Liam, Seth, Todd and Joshua were in a deep discussion about the interpretation of some Scripture verses. It pleased him and he couldn't help but eavesdrop.

"So, the apostle Paul in Ephesians 4 explains that we have to leave the old life we knew and live a life worthy of God. Jesus taught us how to live. We can't just do as we please because the sin we're likely to fall into is always around. It can tempt us to make excuses for those thoughts or behaviour," Joshua expounded with his heart on fire. "We're not ignorant anymore and it's our responsibility to act differently to those who don't confess Jesus as Lord."

"Yeah, I struggle with some things. It's not always easy being a Christian. I have to pray for forgiveness, quite a lot." Todd winced as he mentioned his thoughts, and Seth broke into the conversation.

"I understand what you're saying, Josh. Can I share something with you, and you can tell me if I'm on the right track?"

"Sure, Seth. Go for it."

"Well, I kind of think of analogies on the farm to help understand the Scriptures. You know, being a farmer and all."

They smiled. Of course, that made sense.

"When I'm fencing, I think of those verses. I take down the old, rusty wire and damaged posts then replace them with new, clean and strong ones. I think it's a bit like that, you know, taking off the old ways we live and putting on the new life we have in Jesus. God makes us stronger when we do that and gives us the power to overcome when we struggle. He becomes like the strainer post, solid and firm. We can trust in Him to help hold us up."

"That's exactly right, Seth. We need to be honest and truthful to ourselves and ..."

Joshua's voice continued quietly in the background and Bob's mind rested easy. He could only explain the sudden peace that filled him as knowing and accepting God's will. It was right for him to let this young man help him and he knew he could do it now. The Bishop would be pleased.

Guests said their farewells, thanked Annie and headed off home. The party debris had been cleaned up with help from everyone and Tom said goodnight.

"Don't stay up too long, love. You must be exhausted. I'm off to bed."

"I just need a quiet cup of tea and I'll put the rubbish out."

"I'll do it."

"No, it's okay. You head off to bed."

He nodded and gave her a quick peck on the cheek. Tom was usually in bed by now, and Annie knew he'd be snoring as soon as his head hit the pillow. She needed a bit of time to wind down before she'd be able to sleep. Her tea was hot and she sat with her feet up on the couch. The quiet seeped through her allowing taut muscles to relax. Ten minutes later, she picked up the rubbish bag, and the torch to check on the kids in the tent before retiring. They were all sound asleep.

"Mum," a whispered call.

Annie was confused as she looked at the children, none of them were awake. A movement behind her caught her attention. She turned. Freya stood before her. Annie dropped the torch and threw her arms around her daughter.

"Freya, oh, my Freya. You're back."

"I've been at Grandma Delia's for a couple of months."

"She didn't tell me that when I rang her."

"No, I asked her not to. I had some serious stuff to deal with, and I needed time."

Hot tears poured down Annie's face as she wiped them away with the palm of her hand.

"Mum, I'm truly sorry for all the trouble I've caused you. I'm here to stay if you'll have me."

"Of course, you know we will. You'll be here for Kaimarie's birthday tomorrow. I wish you could've seen her cut the cake and heard the dedication ceremony we had for her."

"I didn't miss out, Mum. I saw and heard it all."

"What? Where were you? How long have you been here?"

Annie's questions tumbled out over the top of each other.

"When I realised there were people here I crept up to the bike shed the long way around and waited in the shadows for ages. It was you I wanted to see first. I got dropped off at the gate earlier and walked up the driveway in the dark. My case is in the bus shelter, but I'll get it tomorrow."

"My very own Freya." Annie placed her hands on either side of her daughter's face. Freya smiled, that was her Mum, the wonderful forgiving mother that she'd thought was lost to her. The smile was gentle and Annie's heart missed a beat. Her girl was back. Annie put her arms out and embraced Freya – her prodigal daughter had come home. At last.

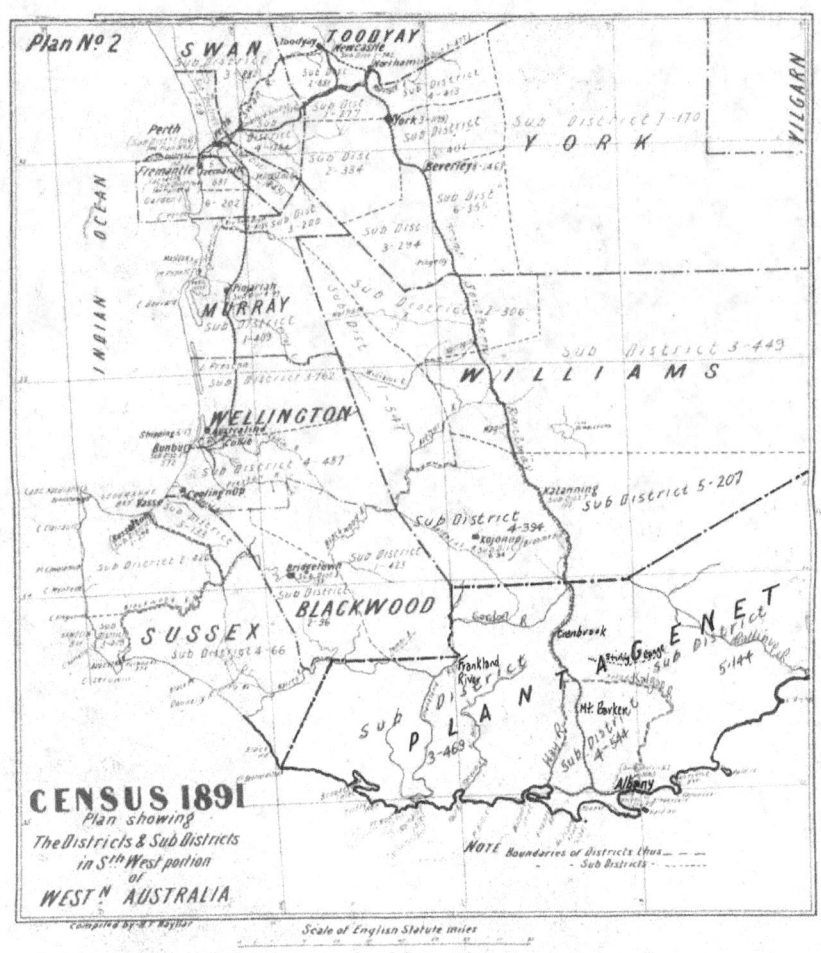

**PLANTAGENET DISTRICT IN WESTERN AUSTRALIA
AS AT CENSUS 1891**

AFTERWORD

Historical Information

The Plantagenet Shire is located in the Great Southern of Western Australia.

It is a rural shire surrounding the town of Mount Barker, near Albany, and was named by early English settlers who often used royal titles.

Plantagenet (n.)

English royal house which reigned from 1154 to 1485 (Henry II to Richard III), emerged from the nickname of Geoffrey, Count of Anjou, who wore a sprig of broom, L. planta genista, in his cap.

Planta genista – linifolia

An erect narrow-leaf shrub bearing yellow flowers
Prolific in the south-west of Western Australia
Introduced from Europe in the 1800's

Footnote references:

1. **Cranbrook** is located 330 kms south-east of Perth. It began in 1889 as a railway siding, named by the Hon. JA Wright, Commissioner of Railways and Director of Public Works, who was in charge of construction of the railway station. He had been born in Cranbrook, in the English county of Kent. Cranbrook proudly promotes itself as 'The Gateway to the Stirlings'. It is a small service centre for the surrounding sheep and cattle properties with wheat silos and grain loading facilities. It is an ideal starting point for exploring the Heritage Listed Stirling Range National Park. The Cranbrook Wildflower Walk displays spectacular native flora in the spring and is located on Salt River Road, 300m past the entrance to the Stirling Range National Park.

2. **Saint Oswald's Anglican Church** had its foundation stone laid on 1st February, 1918 by the Venerable Archdeacon Louch of Albany, assisted by the Reverend Henry G. Barnacle, Rector of Mount Barker – of which the Parish of Cranbrook was a part. A record of the proceedings, a copy of the parish magazine and coins of the realm were deposited in a cavity prepared for this purpose. The contract for the building was given to Mr Jack Haese of Mt Barker, but the work was carried out by Mr Davies, his son Ray and grandson Gordon, from Albany. Stone was quarried two miles south-east of Cranbrook on the property later owned by Mr Ron Lathwell. The first service was held on 10th March, 1918, when 60 people were present at Evensong. The consecration was in November, 1919 with the Bishop of Bunbury, Dr Cecil Wilson. The wood carving on the altar and choir stalls was done by Reverend Barnacle. The church

building was extended when it became too small for the needs of the district. The vestry and extension of the nave was consecrated on Sunday 12th November, 1978 by Bishop Stanley Goldsworthy.

3. **Cranbrook Memorial Hall** is located on the north side of Gathorne Street between Gordon Street and Dunn Street. The Art Deco style building opened on 31st August, 1957.

4. **Bluff Knoll** is the highest peak in the Stirling Range and is 1,099 metres above sea level and is one of only a few places to experience some light snowfall in Western Australia. The trail first drops down to a creek and then goes across a mountainside to a saddle. Here you can look over the ridge to the south coast. The trail then scales the heights to the summit with outstanding 360-degree views. Eucalypt woodland, banksia and grass trees blanket the lower slopes while exposed outcrops higher up reveal layers in the rock.

5. **Stirling Range** is a Heritage Listed National Park boasting 15 peaks over 900m and 50 peaks above 600m of jagged cliffs, sheltered gullies and superb panoramic views. It is the only significant mountain range in the southern half of Western Australia. There are over 1,500 unique species of flora, many of which grow nowhere else in the world.

6. **Stirling's Ridge Walk** follows an ill-defined trail over the spectacular mountain peaks between Bluff Knoll and Ellen's Peak. It takes three days to complete the walk, and hikers should have good navigation skills and be prepared for steep rock and changeable,

if not, severe weather conditions. The Ridge Walk is the only sub-alpine walk in Western Australia and is more of a climb than a walk. It is undoubtedly one of the most spectacular and rewarding walks but it is also a dangerous and difficult one.

7. **Stirling Range Banksia** or Banksia Solandri is a large woody shrub that occurs only in the Stirling Range in the south-west of Western Australia. Its scientific name honours the botanist Daniel Solander. It grows to four metres with large, broad serrated leaves and thick finely-furred stems. Flowering is in spring and early summer. The inflorescences are fawn in colour. Similarly, Dryandra montana grows to 2.5 metres, has hairy stems, linear pinnatisect leaves with twisted, triangular lobes, yellow flowers in heads of about sixty and reddish-brown follicles. It has been declared as Rare Flora and Critically Endangered. This status is due to the loss of habitat because of the soil-borne pathogen, Phytopthora cinnamomi (PC) - commonly known as dieback, two intense fires in quick succession and rarity of seedlings after the fires. Only four populations are known on summits above 900m above sea level, on sandstone and quartzite in dense heath and thicket – the only such habitats in the state.

8. **The Cranbrook Bell** or Darwinia meeboldii is a shrub which is endemic to Cranbrook and the Stirling Range area. It has an erect and straggly habit, growing to between 0.5 and 3 metres high. The bracts around the flowers form a pendant bell which is usually white with red tips. A group of eight small flowers are concealed inside. These are primarily produced in spring between August and November.

Sources:

Source: https://www.aussietowns.com.au/
town/cranbrook-wa#history

Source: http://southernrangesanglicanparish.simplesite.com

Source: http://albanyregion.com.au/bluff-knoll

Source: https://parks.dpaw.wa.gov.au/site/
bluff-knoll-car-park-trail-head

Source: https://www.trailhiking.com.au/
stirling-range-ridge-traverse/

Source: https://en.wikipedia.org/wiki/Banksia_solandri

Source: http://anpsa.org.au/dryandraSG/dryandra67.pdf

Source: https://en.wikipedia.org/wiki/Banksia_montana

Source: https://en.wikipedia.org/wiki/Darwinia_meeboldii

COMING SOON...

Miranda wanted to rail at her mother, but knew it would be a futile exercise. They'd trudged along this well-worn path before, and Miranda begged Wendy to deal with the regret that haunted her.

The peaceful northern beaches of Sydney belies the bitterness and deep anxiety of the woman in the plush house at Little Manly Beach. A challenge from her daughter leaves her reeling. Wendy's fear in facing a future without Miranda forces her into a daring new situation. Will she travel over 4,000 kilometres to country Western Australia?

She's barely even left the house for a decade. Changes are afoot; demands are put upon her. Wendy needs to recognise the truth she has been ignoring once and for all. Book Three in the Plantagenet Trilogy continues to reveal the tales of the much-loved characters from *Courtney's Keys* and *Seth's Solace*.

www.ingramcontent.com/pod-product-compliance
Lightning Source LLC
Chambersburg PA
CBHW071148260626
47162CB00003B/959